Pearl Sydenstricker B
Virginia and taken t
before the turn of the century. The daughter
of Presbyterian missionaries, she lived with
her family in a town in the interior instead of
the traditional missionary compound. Buck
grew up speaking Chinese as well as English
and received most of her education from her
mother. She received an M.A. from Cornell
and taught English literature in several
Chinese universities before she was forced to
leave the country in 1932 because of the revo-
lution.

She wrote eighty-five books and is the most
widely translated American author to this
day. She has been awarded the Pulitzer Prize,
the William Dean Howells Award, and the
Nobel Prize for Literature. She died in 1973.

"Pearl's fiction gave voice to those who had
not been heard, and succeeded in credibly
dramatizing people and places that had been
unknown and alien to most of her readers.
She had, that is to say, a gift for making the
strange seem familiar"

—Peter Conn

Ms. Buck tells us that East and West can meet
on the ground of affectionate understanding
and that human similatities can prevail over
the gulf between cultures.

—Elizabeth Janeway

Other Novels by Pearl S. Buck

All Men Are Brothers (*translator*)
Dragon Seed
East Wind: West Wind
The Good Earth
A House Divided
Imperial Woman
Kinfolk
The Living Reed
Mandala
The Mother
Pavilion of Women
Peony
The Promise
Sons
Three Daughters of Madame Liang

THE NEW YEAR

a novel

Pearl S. Buck

MOYER BELL
Kingston, Rhode Island & Lancaster, England

Published by Moyer Bell

**LIBRARY OF CONGRESS
CATALOGING IN PUBLICATION DATA**

Buck, Pearl S. (Pearl Sydenstricker), 1892-1973. The new year / Pearl S. Buck.

256 p.   22 cm.
1. Domestic fiction. I. Title.
PS3503.U198N4   2007
813'.52—dc22   2007005123
                                  CIP
ISBN 978-155921-391-2 pb

Printed in the United States of America
Distributed in North America by Midpoint Trade Books,
27 West 20th Street #1102, New York, NY 10011 and
in the United Kingdom, Eire, and Europe by
Gazelle Book Services Ltd.,
White Cross Mills, High Town,
Lancaster LA1 1RN England,
1-44-1524-68765, www.gazellebooks.co.uk

THE NEW YEAR

I

THE TELEPHONE RANG.

"Now, what—" Greta muttered.

She smoothed her small white apron and took the receiver. The voice of her mistress sounded clear and musical in her ear.

"Good morning, Greta. I'm still in New York. Is Mr. Winters downstairs yet?"

"No, Mrs. Winters, he's upstairs yet."

"Well, he isn't to come down, Greta. Or if he does, he's not to go out. The doctor called me last night and told me that he has a bad case of influenza. He's to stay in bed and drink liquids all day."

"Mrs. Winters, I can't keep Mr. Winters in bed. He won't stay put. You coming home today like you said—not?"

"I was, Greta, but I can't. The pharmacologists are meeting today and I must fill in on the panel for a man who can't be here."

"Yes, Mrs. Winters."

The pleasant voice flowed on over the wires. "So you must keep him in bed, Greta."

9

"I'll sure try, but—oh, my, here he comes a'ready!" She turned toward the door. "Mr. Winters, Mrs. Winters wants you should talk with her."

"Good," Christopher Winters said. "That's the way to start the morning." He took the receiver and burst into a fit of coughing before he could go on. His wife's voice was reproachful at his ear.

"Darling, you sound worse!"

"No, I'm better."

"Where are you going today? Can't you stay in?"

"Not possible. Berman is coming after breakfast, and we're going to headquarters immediately."

"Have you seen the doctor?"

"Last night."

"Call me, will you, darling? I'll be back at the hotel by seven o'clock. I'm taking the first flight if you don't give a good account of yourself."

"I'll be all right."

"Chris!"

"Yes, my dear?"

"Are you sure you know how much I love you?"

"Haven't you told me?"

"I try to, every day."

"Then I know. Because I know how much I love you."

"I like knowing, the first thing in the morning."

"Silly!"

He hung up so that she would not hear his next fit of coughing. In spite of his declaration of health he felt miserable enough so that he had not dressed as usual before breakfast. Instead, after a shave and shower he had slipped into his old brown wool bathrobe. He sat down now at the table and drank the big glass of orange juice, wincing as the acid poured down his inflamed throat.

"Coffee, Greta," he commanded.

"Right now. You sure got a bad cold, Mr. Winters—not?"

"No worse than yesterday. Has the mail come?"

"I'll go see."

She filled his cup with steaming coffee from the silver pot and went to the front door. Most of his mail went to his law offices, but today, among the letters addressed to Mrs. Christopher Winters II, there was one addressed to him. It was a thin envelope and it bore a foreign stamp. She took the letters to the table.

"Here it is, Mr. Winters. There's one for you. How about I have the stamp? What country is it now, I wonder?"

He took the bluish-gray envelope. "It's from Korea."

"Korea? You know somebody there?"

"Well, hardly. But I was there some twelve years ago, in the Korean War."

"Is that a fact! You like it there maybe now, Mr. Winters?"

"No—well, yes and no. I was glad to come home."

"Was you and Mrs. Winters married already?"

"Yes. Three days. Where's my bacon and eggs?"

"Oh, my!"

She flew off, her apron strings fluttering, and he looked closely at the envelope. There was a Korean name in the upper left-hand corner. Kim—Kim what? Water somewhere had blotted the rest of it. He slit the envelope with his butter knife, drew out a thin sheet of rice paper, and unfolded it. Upon the paper the words were written crudely, but in English. He caught the heading—

"Dear American Father—"

The next line was clear. "My mother talk I not write you never."

He knew instantly. He put the letter down and covered it with the others. Greta was coming in with his bacon and eggs.

"Thank you, Greta," he said.

She left the room and he was alone again. He must keep calm. He did not uncover the letter. Instead he began to eat, deliberately lingering over his plate. It was, of course, perfectly possible. The child had been only a month old when he was shipped out. He had done his best to stay. Let him give himself that credit!

"Don't cry, Soonya. Don't cry, sweet!"

He could hear his own voice, young and agonized, echoing across the years into this quiet dining room in his beautiful home, where he and Laura had been happy, in spite of never having had a child. Had been happy? They were happy now and would continue in happiness, world without end. But the room faded away and what he had supposed was buried forever rose into monstrous reality. Incredible that he could have been so foolish! At twenty-four—even at twenty-four he should have known better . . . even allowing for that sudden transference from one world to another. He had been born here in Philadelphia, as his father and grandfather had been before him, in this handsome old house just off Rittenhouse Square, sheltered, he supposed—at least there had been nothing to prepare him for the swift propulsion into that most ancient country of Asia. So quickly had the summons come that he had no time for preparation or meditation; six months of basic training, then orders for his battalion to bolster the last bitter fight in Korea.

Yet he had been lucky. He had been thrown into battle just before the final mopping up; then an armistice had been declared and he had had time on his hands, time to be lonely and homesick. He had written to Laura and she had replied, but the letters had not been comforting. They were desperately in love, of course; but he did not know when he would get home, he did not know how to tell her about his strange distant life, nor how from his distance even to imagine hers. The memory of their brief marriage had faded into fear, the old fear that he had before the wedding day. Was it fear of Laura or of marriage itself? He didn't know. They were married. Yet there had been times when he was lying in the mud, his rifle ready, every nerve alert against sudden death, when he had wondered if that wedding had ever really taken place, that golden noonday wedding and the three honeymoon days before he'd had to leave. Everything had become indefinite to him except the gray grim mountains of Korea, the damp cold of unending winter and the desolation after war. He told himself again and again that he should be glad that he was alive, and he was not glad. In the midst of the fearful poverty, the ruined people, the lost children, those young American men, he only one of many, were afflicted with misery, surrounded by misery, and could not escape. The cessation of war had taken away even the relief of action.

At last, in despair, he had yielded to the common behavior.

"Aw, come along, kid," his fellows had pleaded and coaxed. "You can't just sit here in the barracks all night by yourself. What are you waitin' for? It's only fun. We're goin' out on the town."

It had been innocent enough at first, the dance hall, no more than a shed thrown up among the ruined buildings of Seoul, the lights unshaded bulbs hanging from the roof, benches lining the walls, a broken piano pounding out the rhythms of rock-and-roll. Everyone was dancing; with every man in uniform was a slim Korean girl, most of them in sleazy Western dress but a few in the wide skirts and short bodices of their own culture. He had dropped down on a bench that night, only to watch, he told himself. The last time he had danced it had been on his honeymoon; Laura, his partner, in his arms, closer to each other than they had ever been before.

What innocence was his that day when he had told her goodbye! Then he had been thrown into skirmish and battle, had climbed the steep Korean mountains to fight hand to hand against the enemy that sprang at him from rock and gully. Of death and dangers he soon knew much, but of love he had only a memory.

He sat there in the dance hall, lost and lonely, and Tom Sullivan, his buddy, had come by—Tom, at whose side he had fought and whose life he had once saved when he had carried him, wounded, down a mountainside, the blood flowing over them both until the doctor in the rough shed at the base had not known whose blood it was.

"Get on your feet, man," Tom had shouted at him that evening. "I've found you a girl. Soonya, meet Chris. Chris, meet Soonya!"

Tom had galloped off with his own partner, a square-faced girl in a tight red dress, and he, Christopher, had been compelled to get to his feet, awkward and shy.

"Dance?" he had muttered.

Soonya had smiled, a sweet, frightened smile, and he had reluctantly taken her in his arms. She wore a pink brocaded skirt, long and full in the Korean fashion, and a short-waisted white silk bodice. In a few minutes he perceived that she knew nothing about dancing. She was not tall, a slight girl, though not as starving thin as most of them were in those days, and she was pretty. Few of the others were really pretty, as he had already noticed, but Soonya was fine-featured, her skin pearly white, her eyes brown and big under soft brown brows. Her little hands were boneless. Yes, even now, years later, he remembered her hands, as tender as a child's, her right hand in his left as they danced, and then later, both her hands in his. She spoke very little English. It was that, perhaps, which had led so soon to caresses. It became necessary to communicate and they had no language.

"How old are you?" he had asked.

For there was no use in trying to keep on dancing. She had no sense of rhythm, at least of Western rhythm. Later, it had seemed then much later, but perhaps it had been only a few days, he learned that she loved music, for she sang Korean songs to him, gentle winding melodies, her fingers plucking at the strings of a lute.

"Old?" she had echoed. "Ah, yes."

She held up ten fingers and then eight. So she was eighteen to his twenty-four.

"You?" she inquired.

He held up the appropriate number of fingers and for the first time they laughed together. He bought her a bottle of Coke and she had not been prepared for the sting in her nose. She had never been here before, then? He could not make her understand his question, but Tom, passing by, had dropped to the bench for a moment's rest. The hall was hot and the air close with the reek of kimchee.

"This one is Dolly," he announced, pointing a thumb at his girl. "It's not her real name. I can't pronounce it. I just call her my baby doll. She's Dolly from now on."

"Tha's right," Dolly said, showing all her teeth in a great laugh.

"She dances real good," Tom went on. "Thanks to me, that is. She sure was a clodhopper at first. Weren't you, kid?"

Dolly laughed. "Tha's right!"

"Cheerful, ain't she? Well, I like that. Soonya will brighten up after she learns some English. It's Soonya's first time, ain't it, Dolly?"

"She come small village yesterday," Dolly explained brightly.

They drifted away again and he was left with Soonya. What attracted him even then was her difference. She was shy, she had avoided the first accidental touch of his hand, and they sat in silence. He watched the dancers, always conscious of the small quiet figure at his side, yet determined not to look at her while he struggled with his own indecision. Was it true that what one did in Asia made no difference at home in America? Did it not make a difference at least to the man himself? Could Tom, for example, also newly married before he left home in Centerville, Nebraska, go back the same man he had been before he took up life in a shack here—a hooch, they called it—with Dolly?

"Who cares if I don't tell 'em?" Tom had said. "East is East and West is West, as the saying goes. Dolly knows there can't be anything serious. I'm married. She knows that."

The dust and heat of the hall had become intolerable. He stole a look at Soonya. She was waiting for the look and she smiled at him again. He rose, wondering what to do with her. Tom and Dolly drifted by in a tight clinch.

"Where you off to, boy?" Tom asked.

"Anywhere," he said. "It's stifling in here."

"Less go hooch," Dolly put in. "I make chow."

He had hesitated but there could be no harm in going to Tom's hooch for an hour or so. He would not stay, of course.

"Mr. Winters, here's Mr. Berman." Greta's voice brought him abruptly back to Philadelphia. He put the foreign envelope under the pile of letters.

"Show him in, Greta."

He drank his coffee and set the cup down empty as a burly figure appeared at the door.

"How's the future governor of our fair state feeling this morning?" he shouted.

"Sit down, Joe," Christopher said. "Greta, another cup of coffee."

"Thanks." Berman's voice, hoarse, enthusiastic, overpowered the room. He drew a clutch of papers from his briefcase. "Guess what? Polls! A landslide! Public opinion all for you, the Honorable Christopher Winters, leading attorney of our fair city."

"Joe, for God's sake, stop horsing around."

"I'm not! I'm telling the truth. We've been conducting a private poll—movies, supermarkets, and so forth—crowds. There's no doubt. You've cleaned up the city—now it's the state—they need you—man of ideals—everything! We'll lick the machine, Governor Winters! Sounds good, don't it? The people are for you. Well, cheer up. Don't you like the news?"

A fit of coughing prevented his reply. Berman was instantly sympathetic. "Boy, you do have some cold. Take care of yourself, boy."

"I am doing so. In fact, I've just promised my wife that I wouldn't leave the house today."

Joe Berman's jowls dropped. "What'll I do about the delegation from the women's clubs? Eleven o'clock this morning."

Christopher Winters sighed. "I'd forgotten. All right, I'll come."

"I don't want to be blamed, now. Your wife's a powerful—"

"Ridiculous!"

"Oh, now, I don't mean she isn't charming, a very beautiful lady, perfect for a governor's wife. Do you realize, Chris, where this will lead? Governor to White House!"

"We'll see. Now clear out, will you? Go on over to headquarters and tell them I'll be there in an hour."

"Okay, boy."

The room subsided into quiet after his boisterous departure. Christopher drew out the gray envelope from among the others and slipped it into the pocket of his bathrobe. Greta came in with fresh coffee.

"Put the mail on the desk in my study, will you, Greta?" he directed. "I'll take my coffee up to the dressing room."

"You ain't going out, Mr. Winters!"

"Yes, I am."

"Mrs. Winters told me not to let you go out. What'll she say when she comes home tonight?"

He gave her a wink. "Tell her you had to take my orders. Obey me or get fired!"

"Yes, sir," she chuckled, "but you hadn't ought to go, Mr. Winters. She's absolutely right."

Upstairs in his dressing room he took the letter from his pocket. Should he read it now and distress himself all day? Yet the crux of decision was not whether to read the letter. It was how to tell Laura—if he must tell her. That was the real question. Should she be told? Must she be told? His head was beginning to ache again, vilely. He had a fit of coughing that seemed endless. The room whirled about his head. He should never have told Berman that he was coming to the headquarters' offices. It was impossible—the doctor was right—Laura was right—he must stay in bed. He sank upon the bed and reached for the telephone on the bedside table.

"Darling, how are you feeling?"

He was wakened by Laura's clear voice, by her cool hand on his forehead. He opened his eyes, dazed by sleep. "Greta says she came upstairs and found you'd gone back to sleep. She says you've been sleeping all day. You sounded so awful this morning I could scarcely wait to leave my pharmacologists and get home."

"I feel pretty miserable."

He tried not to sound self-pitying and was aware that he did. He rolled over on his back, stretched, and smoothed his hair.

"It came over me all at once," he went on. "I finished my breakfast and Berman dropped in and I thought I'd be all right. Then when I climbed the stairs I was suddenly— well, just all in."

"It's the way this flu goes," Laura said.

She leaned to kiss him but he turned his head. "Don't— I'm contagious."

"Oh, nonsense. I never get anything."

She caught his head between her hands and kissed him full on the mouth. He laughed, comforted in spite of himself.

"Perseverance is one of your more trying traits."

She looked suddenly wistful. "Is it, Chris? I've wondered sometimes. But I never catch colds. I've always been so disgustingly healthy. My two brothers got things when we three were small together, but never I. It used to make them hate me."

He felt better. "Now it's my turn to say 'Nonsense.' "

He sat up, reached for her and pulled her to his breast, his lips on the soft nape of her neck. Surely he could tell her, surely they loved each other well enough for him to tell her. Where had he put the letter? Ah yes, in the pocket of his bathrobe! But his bathrobe—it was lying there where he had tossed it across the back of a chair. What if she—

"Hand me my bathrobe, sweet," he said. "I'll get up. I feel much better, now that you're home."

"I don't think you should."

"No, really. I'll—just give me my bathrobe, will you?"

Did she notice the edge in his voice? She rose obediently and brought the bathrobe to him. He put it around his shoulders. Under the bedcovers he felt for the pocket. Yes, the letter was still there. Of course he would have to tell her. But he had better read all of it first. What had made him go to bed and sleep for hours without so much as finishing it? What if Greta had come in to straighten the room and hang up his things and it had dropped out . . .

Laura's hand was on his forehead again. "You have fever. Do let me ask the doctor—"

In his relief he was suddenly amenable. "Tell you what —you take my temperature. If I have fever you are right. Otherwise, I'm right. Compromise?"

She laughed. "You're a good politician. I've always known it."

She rose as she spoke, going toward the bathroom medicine closet, and her voice trailed off. It began again as she entered the room, shaking down the thermometer and peering at it under the light.

"I could have done with some of your competitive skill today."

"Tell me," he mumbled, as she thrust the thermometer into his mouth. In his enforced silence she spoke rapidly.

"Well, as you know, I'm not satisfied with the last third of the book. Wilton is far too sure of his conclusions. I can't agree that we have reached any area of certainty with these sea plant drugs. I'm a scientist before I'm a writer, and I simply don't believe that you can test human brain tissue by experiments upon animal brain tissue."

He muttered around the thermometer. "Aren't we all animals?"

She scolded him but tenderly. "Now you'll have to begin over again. Let me talk, will you? I so seldom get the chance!"

He opened his eyes wide in mischievous question and she insisted, laughing.

"It's true-true-true! You're twice as articulate as I am and you know it. You always say the right thing, darn you—and it's another reason why I love you! Oh Chris—"

She subsided, her head on his breast. He smoothed her bright hair, her lovely hair, red gold—

"I love you so terribly," she whispered. "I love you so that it hurts me to speak of it . . . I can hear your heart beating—under my cheek. Why is it so fast? It's a broken beat . . . Chris, do you feel really ill? Is there something you're not telling me?"

She lifted her head. Her dark eyes, stone gray but warm under dark lashes, were searching his face. He was glad of the thermometer in his mouth, so that he need not answer. She took it out, forgetting her question. But how could she have guessed there was something to tell? Of course she had not—

"Oh, you do have fever—over a hundred! Indeed you shall not get up. I'll have my dinner served up here with you."

He sat up abruptly and snatched the thermometer out of his mouth. "I hate eating in bed. A hundred is nothing, darling. And this room is hot. We'll compromise. I'll take a quick shower, put on fresh pajamas and my velvet dressing gown, and we'll dine downstairs. I want to hear everything. I want to tell you everything. Berman says things are swell at the office. Some sort of poll—I want to tell you. He'll be calling up—"

"He has called a dozen times, Greta says. He wants to come over this evening, but I said we'd have to see."

"Right. But the way I'm feeling now, I want to see him. Things are piling up. The next few weeks ought to tell the story."

She rose, docile as usual when she knew he had made up his mind. He had to say that for her. He was master in his own house and she wanted him to be. He had a theory that a strong woman wanted a strong man. On the other hand, he didn't want a weak woman. He'd always known that Berman, for example—

"A penny," Laura said, lingering.

He recalled himself. "What? Oh, just foolishness. I was thinking about Berman. I distrust him in spite of myself. I don't know whether I should make him my campaign manager."

"He worships you."

"I was thinking about his wife—"

She laughed and sat down again on the edge of the bed beside him. "Oh, come now—his wife? What has she to do with it?"

He joined her laughter. "Sounds stupid, doesn't it? But—"

"She's stupid, if that's what you mean."

"That's the point. Isn't it proof of a weakness somewhere in Berman that he married a stupid little moron? He orders her around like a servant. He does that because he needs to, doesn't he?"

"Are you judging a man by the woman he married?"

"Of course. I count it the best proof of my own manhood that I married you."

"Oh, Chris, really!"

"No, I mean it. You're glorious, Laura. But you're—well, it takes courage to marry a woman like you."

To his surprise, he saw her lower lip tremble. He knew the sign. She did not weep easily, but she could be inexplicably and easily hurt.

"Now, darling," he said hurriedly, and reached for her hand. "I've said something wrong. What I mean is that I'm proud of myself that I want a woman like you. It takes a real man to match you, doesn't it? Aren't you proud of yourself as a woman? You could never have married a small man, could you? Of course not. We measure ourselves by each other, don't we? We're well mated. I'm not a whit behind you. I even think I'm good enough for you. How's that for conceit?"

She was in his arms now, half-laughing, half-sobbing. "O, Chris, you'd convince me of anything, I do believe! But it's true I'm happy, so happy with you. Still, I know I'm frightening. I can't help it, can I? Brains have nothing to do with sex, have they? We take what we are, because we can't help it."

She freed herself from his arms, gently but suddenly. He knew what she was thinking. In the days when they still thought they could have children, when it did not occur to them that they could not, they had spoken of the children they would have together, the splendid children, compounded of his dark good looks and her golden beauty and their brains combined, those children who were not yet born and now would never be. Man and woman, they were so wholly one that it seemed incredible to consider an incompatibility deep in their physical beings. They would not give up hope, they had told each other, but he knew that as the years passed, hope was passing, too. At such a moment as this they no longer spoke aloud of children. But he knew what she was thinking when she pulled away from his arms. As for him, he remembered the letter in his pocket. Suddenly it occurred to him that he had fathered a child, a son. Then it was not his fault.

He pushed aside the monstrous thought. She had no fault. Innocent of any fault in her body, she had married him, and she was still innocent. He would never tell her.

Would it not be wrong to tell her? To hurt her as that would hurt?

"I'll be ready in a few minutes," he said.

"I'll change, too," she said, going toward her own room.

In his bathroom, shaving and showering, he considered. For her sake, should he not forever keep secret the boy's existence? The letter was still there in the pocket of his bathrobe, hanging on the back of the door. Perhaps he should destroy it. No, he could not thus quickly decide whether to tell her. If he told her, she would want to see the letter. And must it not be answered? He dried himself carefully, wrapped a towel about him, took the letter out of the pocket.

So Soonya had made the boy promise never to tell him that he had been born! He felt a remembering wave of tenderness. No, he had not forgotten her. She had remained somewhere in his being, a warm presence, not to be compared to his love for Laura, but a presence. Then why had the boy disobeyed his mother? He unfolded the letter and read the next sentence.

"Now I am have no chance for good school."

School? The last time he had seen his son he was one month old. The child had been born in autumn, the result, he thought with a groan, of the winter, cold and gray. In the small hooch, between the thin walls, the only way to keep warm was under the quilt. That icy wind, blowing down from the white reaches of Siberia, over the sharp peaks of the northern mountains, penetrated stone and earth, bone and flesh. The only comfort he had in those days was in the simple closeness of Soonya's body next to his, a primitive comfort, necessary, it had seemed then, to keep him from insanity. Could he explain that to Laura? Could she understand? Could any woman? Even to him now it seemed not wholly explicable. Yet he remembered. And the child—with what dismay he had heard of the child! He had not the courage that day to reveal to Soonya his dismay. Her joy had touched his heart, and he had covered his sorrow with a pretense of joy. That, too, he remembered.

It was spring before she had told him, spring after the winter so fiercely cold. The day was mild, an April day, warm in the sun, but the shadows were chill. They had taken food in a small wooden box, cold rice and kimchee and in his pocket two oranges, and had climbed the mountain beyond the town. The wind was persistent on those steep flanks, and they had searched for a cranny somewhere between rocks, a shelter where the sun could warm them. He had found such a place, and had drawn her into it with him. They sat close together, cushioned upon the dead grass of winter, and he had taken chocolate bars from another pocket. She delighted in chocolate and he had stopped at the PX to buy them for her. Now her conscience smote her.

"No," she said. "Eating rice first. Then sweet is good."

She had a strict sense of duty, working in unexpected ways. Thus she could forbid herself a sweet until a proper time, but she never withheld herself from him. Day or night, if they were alone she yielded joyfully to his demand. She delighted in his love—no, it was not love, was it, and yet who can define the manifold faces of love? Let him confess that he had loved Soonya, not as he loved Laura now with his whole manhood in mind and body, but he had loved her. And since his first experience of physical love, reckless and unabashed, was with Soonya, it had been necessary to become accustomed to loving Laura again. For he had taken it for granted, when he returned, that Laura, too, being a woman, could respond easily and immediately to his sudden need at any hour of day or night once they were alone. When she did not, he was first angry and then wounded. At last, because he knew he could not live without her, he learned that what she gave when she was ready to give was infinitely better, deeper and more satisfying than Soonya's simple readiness, however generous, had been. For Soonya indulged him, but Laura, loving him with full respect, did not and could not.

"It must be right, for your sake as well as mine," she said.

In those Korean days, when Soonya was the only woman he knew, he had been too young to understand the fullness of love between man and woman who are truly mated. It had been chocolate bars and sweetness between meals, and that day on the mountain, Soonya had yielded on all except chocolate bars. They had eaten their cold rice and kimchee and then, while they were eating the chocolate bars, she had told him. She took his hand and placed it over her little bare belly. For at noon it was warm as summer up there between the rocks and she had loosened her bodice and then her skirt at his command, laughing at him while she did so.

"You are so hot man," she had remarked, and then she had put his hand on her belly. "Your baby," she had said. Two simple words, but he fell into a chill. His mouth went dry, his head swam. He opened his mouth to protest and then he saw her face, lit by simple gladness. Now, of course, he knew that she had thought it would mean marriage. That was what they all dreamed of, those girls, even Dolly, for if not Tom, then perhaps another man. But Soonya had been different. Alas, her difference! He had not the heart then to protest. He could only pretend.

"Gee, that's swell," he had muttered in sheer terror.

Why had he been so afraid? Is every man frightened at his own power for reproduction? He simply had not thought of a child. He had supposed that she had ways of prevention. It did not occur to him, in his innocence, that she would allow a child to be born. He had considered only the pleasure she gave, the ability to help him forget where he was—yes, and with whom.

"So swell," she had said, leaning against him in contentment.

But he had not been able to go on with lovemaking. When she perceived the astonishing fact of his inability, she had looked up at him.

"You sick?" she had inquired, with tenderness.

"I'm getting cold," he had said. "We'd better go."

The sun had in fact hidden itself behind gray clouds rising out of the valleys. She had put on her clothes, and, clinging to his hand, had followed him down the mountain. Nor did he enter their little hooch. Instead he kissed her cheek and left her without a word. When he looked back she was standing at the door, gazing after him with a sad puzzlement on her lovely face. He had not gone back to her for five days. Then, unable to endure his loneliness, he had accepted the knowledge of his fatherhood, and he went to her. Only months later, when the child was born, had he known that he must return to his own country. Faced with the choice of return or reenlistment, he knew he had to go back.

When he told her, she clung to him, sobbing, and the child, put down suddenly upon the tatami mat, had wailed with her.

"I must go, Soonya," he had said. "I have my parents." He could not say "my wife." He had never told her he was married.

"Yes, yes, I am knowing your parents first. You come back?"

"I'll try," he had promised, and wished he need not lie. For of course he could never come back.

That last farewell he could not bear, even now, to remember. He had taken a last look at the child, a solemn little creature, with the strangely Asian and yet not Asian face, and it had seemed to him, though of course it was imagination, that the child had met his look with recognition. Certainly it was the only time he had felt a flicker of kinship.

"Beautiful?" Soonya had asked him proudly through her tears.

"Of course, because he's yours." At last he had to tear her arms from about his neck. She had fallen to the floor, crying wildly, but he had not dared to stoop to lift her up again. He had run from the hooch, his own throat too tight for speech.

And now the child was writing to him and calling him "My American Father!"

There was a tap at the door. "Are you all right, Chris?"

Laura's voice, and he answered, thrusting the letter back into the bathrobe pocket, "I'm coming." He put on the velvet dressing gown and opened the door. He had been dawdling among his own thoughts, he told her now, while she had bathed and changed.

"How lovely you look," he said.

"This old dress," she said shyly. She could never accustom herself to his praise.

"You know it's one of my favorites," he reminded her.

It was a black chiffon hostess gown, the sleeves long and full, and the neck low. Her skin was flawless, but if she had a fault it was that she was too thin. Her bones, though delicate, were too obvious. The memory of Soonya sprang suddenly out of the shadows. Soonya had a delicate framework, too, a dainty skeleton, not as tall as Laura's, but clothed in softly rounded flesh. He pushed back the memory resolutely.

"I'm almost ready," he said, rummaging in a drawer for a fresh handkerchief.

"I'll go on down and see if dinner is ready," she said.

He heard her footsteps on the stairs, and sat down to rest for a moment, suddenly weak. The whole thing was a strain, coming in the midst of a hot political campaign. He mustn't take it too seriously. He might just ignore the letter. The boy would think he never got it. No, no, he couldn't do that, not when the child was his son. If Soonya had been like the others, if she had told the boy to write, to beg, he might have refused to take heed. No, even so the child was his. There was, he supposed, some responsibility, moral, that is, not legal. He had, though, heard somewhere that in those Asian countries the father was held responsible for the child. Yes, he'd known that long ago and had forgotten it—purposely? No, surely only unconsciously, since he had not purposely—

There was a tap on the door again. He turned his head. "Yes?"

"It's me, Mr. Winters, Greta. Dinner is served a'ready, Mrs. Winters is waiting—candles lit and all."

"I'm coming," he called.

Five minutes later he was ready. The letter—what should he do with it? It would be safer in his briefcase than in a bathrobe pocket.

He went downstairs. Laura was standing by the chimneypiece in the dining room. The fire was blazing and she made a picture as he glanced through the open door, the light from the flames flickering on her face and bright hair.

"Coming," he called as he passed. "I just want to look at something on my desk."

He went into the study and closed the door. There, alone, he thrust the gray envelope deep among the papers in his briefcase. Then he locked the briefcase and put the key in the inner pocket of his topcoat, hanging in his study closet. Eased and ready for the evening, he joined Laura in the dining room.

At his end of the oval table he listened as she talked, watching her with a remorseful tenderness. She enchanted him and she made him afraid. There were times, such as tonight, when he wondered if any man could understand her variety. At his insistence she had given up the special work she was doing when they first met, that monstrous, incredible task of discovering in the Sargasso Sea those elements which might result in finding new antibiotics in marine algae. She was actually diving into waters so deep that she was using scuba equipment.

"What's scuba?" he had demanded, upon their first meeting, when she told him what she was doing.

"Self-contained, underwater breathing apparatus," she had explained.

He had done some research of his own, then, in private astonishment at her daring, and when he found that if one neglected to breathe in and out normally in the clutches of the monstrous apparatus, one could die of an air bubble in the lungs, he was in a panic until she had promised to work above water. Now she limited herself to a laboratory of her own in collaboration with headquarters at the Institute of Oceanography in New York.

"What did you talk about today at your meeting?" he asked.

"Apart from arguing with Wilton over the book, we spent the whole time still trying to define when and how a sea plant becomes a sea animal," she said. "It doesn't matter, I suppose, and yet it seems wonderful just to think of all life as a continuous stream, no barriers, really, between the species."

"Definition, please!" he demanded.

"Well, some sea plants look green, as plants should, but they swim like animals and they eat like animals—protozoological miracles."

She forgot herself as she always did when she spoke of the science which absorbed her mental life. Her eyes shone, her skin glowed, and he leaned forward to look at her with such pleasure that she blushed and stopped short.

"Now what?" she demanded.

He spoke slowly, his eyes upon her. "While you talk of underwater monstrosities I am remembering a certain day at a fashion show. I was covering the show as a cub reporter during a college vacation and I saw a tall, slim girl, so beautiful that I couldn't breathe. She came walking down the aisle in a white summer frock and a big white hat. Could that girl be you?"

She laughed. "And I remember a handsome, dark young man who sat in the front row, pad on his knees, pencil in hand. And I said to myself that he didn't at all look like a man who'd be interested in fashions or a fashion model, especially one too tall."

"Not too tall for me! I like a tall girl, just so she's not taller than I am. Three inches, I said, and we measured a few weeks later. Three inches, exactly! Whereupon I be-lieve I proposed, didn't I?"

"I was afraid you wouldn't! Oh, we were a silly pair! Do you know that Milgrant is asking me to come back and model again for them this year? Just for fun I might. A young matron, I suppose."

"You didn't tell me for three weeks after we were engaged that you were a scientist."

"I was afraid to."

"Until I said I was looking for a girl with brains."

She put down her knife and fork. "Chris! If we ever stop talking like this—"

"We never will."

"Promise?"

"So help me—"

Greta opened the door, disobeying orders that she was never to appear except between courses. "I have my meals alone with my wife," Chris had always insisted.

"Excuse me, Mr. Winters. It's Mr. Berman."

He looked at his watch. "Oh, well—yes, he's early. Let him have coffee with us."

"Yes, Mr. Winters."

She disappeared and a moment later ushered in Joe Berman, overflowing with good nature and eagerness and ready talk.

"Well, well, our first lady's back from the wilderness of science! Nobody would ever believe it, would they now, to look at you. I mean you're not the dry type, so to speak. Brainy and scrawny, I always say. Hello, Chris. You better?"

"Sit down, Berman," he replied. "Greta's bringing in coffee."

"Well, now, I couldn't have timed it better. How does it feel to be the people's choice? Have you told her?"

"Premature. It's only a poll, Laura."

"Forthcoming events cast their shadows, et cetera," Berman rejoined. He dropped his voice to seriousness as he sat down. "Say, I hope you'll be back in the office tomorrow. Every day counts now. We've got competition in Barrows. He's the old type and people are used to him. As one man says to me today, 'At least we know what his faults are'— Barrows, I mean. They're a little leery about the state being cleaned up."

"Only the machine."

"That's what I mean." He turned heavily to Laura. "But here we are, talking business before the little lady!"

She exchanged a look with Chris and bit her lower lip. He laughed. "Be careful, Joe, you're insulting my wife!"

Berman looked from one to the other. "I don't mean to—I mean—"

"Chris is teasing me," Laura said, calmly. "Pay no heed to him."

She frowned extravagantly at her husband, and he laughed again.

"No, I'm only joking. I tell her everything, Joe, and you know I do. She's given me some of the best advice I've ever had. Fact is, she's probably the one who should be running for governor, only I want the job for myself!"

"I wouldn't be governor if it were handed to me," she said with tranquility. "I'm much too happy as I am."

The telephone rang and she rose. "Excuse me, please. I'm expecting a call from the laboratory."

She rose, the picture of grace, and as she walked past her husband she put out her hand to him. He caught it and kissed the fragrant palm.

"Coming back?"

"Perhaps not. You two will want to talk and I must look over my notes tonight."

"Later, then."

"Yes."

She drifted out of the room and Berman sighed.

"What a first lady she'll make in the White House some day!"

"Yes." Chris's voice was absent-minded, and he rose abruptly.

"Let's have our coffee in my study. I have something to tell you."

"So that is how it happened," he said.

A dying coal fell into the ash. He had lit the fire when they came into his study, for the air was still chilly with early spring. Then he had motioned to Berman to take the chair opposite his own. While the dry apple wood leaped into a blaze he had begun abruptly.

"I have something to tell you before we talk about tomorrow. Strictly speaking, it's my own private business, except that now nothing seems to be simply my own business. I can't catch cold, apparently, without its becoming a public liability. I don't know how to begin, except at the beginning, and tell it straight."

And he began with the day he had landed in Korea and continued until this morning and the arrival of the letter. The blaze died down into a bed of coals, and coals became ash. Berman, moving now and again in his seat, had said nothing until he finished. Then he spoke.

"As you say, it's nobody's business except that now it's

everybody's business. Plenty of young fellows did the same thing and it don't matter. There must be plenty of those half-breed kids, too. I never thought about it, but there must be. Fact is—"

He broke off and rubbed his chin. "Well, that's neither here nor there. I was in Germany, myself . . . Does your wife know?"

"Not yet."

"You going to tell her?"

"I—yes, I suppose so. I don't know just how or when."

"Must you tell her?"

He looked up at Berman sharply. "Must I not?"

They stared into each other's eyes. Berman spoke. "I don't see why you should. Fact is, it would be better if you didn't. Women make a fuss about such things. They never understand how a man can—well, you know how it is with women. They are all the same, when you come right down to it, and the fewer who know it the better. If you don't answer the letter the kid will think you never got it. That's my advice. Tear up the letter and forget it. You never meant to have a kid, did you?"

"Of course not. When I saw him I scarcely felt he was mine."

"Maybe he isn't."

"Yes, he is mine."

"How do you know?"

"She was a virgin."

"Temporary!"

"While I was there, I was the only one."

Silence came between them. They both sat staring into the fire. Berman sighed at last.

"Well, all I can say is, for God's sake keep it quiet! It wouldn't matter if you were an ordinary citizen. Maybe it wouldn't matter too much if you were just an ordinary governor. But you know what the party's dreaming about. You're Presidential timber. Of course you have a long way to go—another year, and then governor for one term at least. After that—well, the sky's the limit, and you know where the sky is. Our people love smut and scandal among themselves, but when they choose a President they want a man with a halo. Even if they know he doesn't deserve it, they want to be able to give it to him. Keep quiet, I say. If the story gets out, you'll have to deal with it, but it'll be something people won't want to believe, and so they won't believe it, so long as you don't confirm it. Of course the other side mustn't get it, either."

He was silent for a minute, then spoke in a lowered voice. "Say—I've always wanted to know—are those Asian women different from—"

Christopher rose, interrupting with a furious gesture, suddenly loathing this man. Then, sickeningly, it occurred to him that he must not antagonize even Berman. The man was necessary, and if offended could now retaliate. He bit off his disgusted retort and sat down again. "Let's talk about tomorrow, shall we? And I'll think over your advice. I half believe you're right—"

In the night, alone in his bed, he knew that Joe Berman was wrong. The pale spring moonlight shone across the room and, sleepless, he saw the warm orange and brown tones of the room fade into ghostly pallor. When he had gone upstairs it was after midnight and Laura was already asleep. He had opened the door between their rooms and had seen her there in her bed, her long hair streaming across the pillow, her hand under her cheek.

"Darling."

He made the call a whisper but she did not waken. Half relieved, half longing, he had closed the door again and had gone to his own bed. For an hour or so he slept. Then he awakened suddenly, as though he had heard a cry. He listened, wondering if it were she. But the house was quiet, except for the creaking of ancient wooden beams. He used to think, when he was a boy sleeping in this very room, that a ghost walked in the night. Now he knew that it was only the house itself, settling into age, creaking in the coolness of the night. He was intolerably, inexplicably lonely. He had brought the briefcase upstairs with him, and it stood here on the floor beside his bed. It was absurd to feel it must be near him. He must do something else with the letter, read it through and then destroy it. But not tonight! He had as much to bear as he could endure alone.

Then as suddenly as he had wakened, he knew he could not even decide alone what he should do. The night magnified monstrously the burden which lay upon him. He might deceive the people, but he had no right to deceive his wife. And suppose he tried to, and in spite of every endeavor, Laura found out? He should never have told Berman, a shifty politician. What would she think of his having told someone else before he told her? How could he answer her eternal question? "Why?" He could hear the question—"Why didn't you tell me?" Why didn't he tell her? How, indeed, could he reveal his secret to Joe Berman, who would infest it with sordid untruth, and not tell Laura, his best friend as well as his wife?

"I can't bear myself," he muttered.

Was he then too great a coward to tell his wife the truth about himself?

"Maybe I am," he muttered.

Still he hesitated. He was sure of her love, sure of her understanding—no, he wasn't, he was not quite sure of any woman's understanding, not even when the woman was Laura. Pity he could not endure, and just now it was not even love that he wanted. He wanted to convey to her somehow that what he had done had not been what he really wanted to do—no, wait, he had only wanted to feel close to another human being. In those days, in the unutterable isolation of war, the separation from all that was normal and good, he needed human warmth, something more profound than the rough comradeship of men. He wanted to be saved from becoming what they were. Somehow Soonya had saved him. Could he make Laura understand that? No no, wasn't this simply asking for compassion? Better to say it bluntly—"I was like the other fellows. I took a girl." Except that he did not believe he was like the other fellows!

In the brief darkness between moonset and dawn, he came to the knowledge of what he must do. When the first faint glimmer of gold on the horizon announced the day, he rose from his bed. He went to his bathroom, brushed his teeth, shaved, took a shower and combed his hair. Then, wrapping himself in his bathrobe, he opened the door of her room. She was sleeping, her face shadowy in the faint morning light. How still she was, her breath coming and going as lightly as a child's, a breath always sweet with health! Her long lashes lay on her cheeks, her right hand was outflung across the bed. He leaned over her and kissed the softly closed lips. She stirred and opened her eyes, she smiled, and without a word, she lifted the silken coverlet. He came into her bed and lay beside her.

"I tried to stay awake last night until you came," she murmured in a child's voice.

"I'm glad you didn't. I was very late."

She turned to him, fitting her body to his, an invitation he understood. It was always her first impulse after disagreement, this invitation which declared the renewal of their basic love. This first, she was saying without words, and all else follows. Now he must deny her, although never before had he denied her, for until he had told her what he had to tell her, to make love would be a sacrilege. But was this invitation in his favor? Would the shock be greater because she was ready for him and he refused to accept it?

He felt the tip of her finger on his lips.

"So silent!" she murmured.

He caught her hand in his and held it against his breast.

"My love, I must tell you something."

And he told her, simply, of what had happened the day before. "While I was at breakfast, Greta brought in the mail. There was a letter for me from Korea—a letter I never expected to get."

He talked on, his words spare and terse, his gaze upon

the ceiling. The brightening dawn stole over the room. He felt her body change. She did not withdraw, not at first, but she lay in a stillness that was intense. When the sun slanted through the newly budding sycamore trees on the street outside the windows, he came to an end. He heard her sigh. Then she sat up and twisted her long hair about her head.

"At least I've told you," he said.

"Of course you had to tell me."

She sat, thinking, her gaze on the windows now lit with sunlight. He saw her profile, grave and thoughtful, and he waited.

"I wish you hadn't told Berman," she said.

"Sooner or later, he had to know. Perhaps I should have waited until I'd told you. But if he'd said at once last night that there was no use in going on with this election, then I'd have told you that, too."

She seemed not to hear this. She mused, her voice far away. "I'd rather you didn't tell him that I know."

"I won't," he promised.

"Because," she went on, "I cannot bear to speak of it to him, or hear him speak of it. Or have between us the silence of not speaking."

"I know. It's between you and me now, really."

She turned on him sharply. "What do you mean—it's between you and me *now?* It's always been, hasn't it? Just because I didn't know—"

"I should have told you long ago. About the girl, I mean. But it seemed so dead and forgotten."

"Forgotten, perhaps, but not dead. There's a living child."

"Do you want to see the letter?"

She considered that, too. "No," she said at last. "At least, not yet. The child doesn't seem important just now. It's—the woman."

"Oh, Laura—no, she's not—"

He pulled her down to him, but she freed herself.

"No, please, Chris. Let me think."

He threw aside the covers. "I'll leave you to yourself," he said gently.

He wished she would protest but she did not. She followed him with her eyes, large and thoughtful, and when he paused at the door, unable to part from her in such suspense, she tried to smile. He came back in a rush.

"Darling, darling, all these years we've been married—they count, don't they?"

"Oh, yes," she agreed. "Oh, certainly. Nothing can take them away. It's just that I—the question is, of course—"

He sat down on the edge of the bed, forbidding himself the impulse to crush her in his arms. "What is the question?"

"I don't quite know. Perhaps I can't know until I have the answer. Someone said that—who was it?"

"Gertrude Stein, when she was dying."

"Oh, yes, how could I forget? Such wonderful last words! 'What is the answer?' When no one spoke she said: 'Then what is the question?' "

"Stop talking, Laura. You're just wasting time."

"I know it, and I need time."

"We both do. Let's go ahead with our day. We'll both be thinking. When we meet, we'll exchange our thoughts."

She looked at him with bright and empty eyes and nodded as though she had not heard. He made his voice stern.

"Laura, you are not to forget that I love you and only you. I will not allow you to separate yourself from me. If you leave me I shall simply come after you. Wherever you are, I'll find you and stay there with you, if I can't bring you back. As long as I live you'll never escape me, because I shall be there. Do you hear me?"

She nodded, but he refused the gesture.

"Answer me," he insisted. "Do you hear me?"

"Yes," she said. "I hear you, Chris."

"I hope your wife will campaign with you," Henry Allen said.

"I cannot say," he replied.

He had scarcely arrived at his office after his lonely breakfast—for Laura had sent word by Greta that he was not to wait for her—when Berman came in, ruffling his spiky hair in excitement, to announce that the city's richest man, Henry Allen, a banker of old Quaker ancestry, was in the front office asking if Mr. Winters was in.

"Are you?" Berman demanded.

"Of course I am," he had replied.

Now, here in one of his easy chairs, the old man sat facing him. Everyone knew the tall, stooped figure, the head of a family which lived with ostentatious simplicity in one of the oldest and largest mansions in the county.

For nearly an hour they had talked, he listening except to reply to Henry Allen's plain questioning.

"I like your program," Henry Allen concluded. "I particularly like the boldness of the tax and budget reforms. They are much needed." He spoke slowly and precisely, exactly the sort of voice suited to his gray and colorless being. "But in declaring yourself thus, it will be a help if your good wife can be at your side. I am told that she is interested in oceanography."

"Quite true," Christopher said. "She is second in command at the Institute in New York."

"Then she is away from home a good deal?"

"On the contrary. She is writing a book on her nearly completed research, so she's only occasionally away—yesterday, for example—for a conference, or to check some point."

"Then she is free to join you?"

"I am sure she will do all she can to help me."

"You have children?"

The casual question which once he would have answered so lightly in the negative suddenly appeared impossible to answer at all. He hesitated too long and then replied too abruptly.

"We have no children."

"Regrettable," Henry Allen said. "I think it always helps for a public figure to have a family. I myself have six children, all of them sons. Not that I ever contemplated going into public life, but as a banker it has been useful to be surrounded with a family. There is an element of stability."

"It is regettable that we have no children," he agreed.

Henry Allen rose. "Well, I see I have been here an hour. I will delay you no longer. I would like to declare myself in your favor and to offer you my resources, such as they are."

Christopher rose, in turn, his hand outstretched. "I can't thank you enough, Mr. Allen. If you will join my group of advisers, I'll be most glad."

"At my age," Henry Allen said with a small, pale smile, "there is little left that one can do except advise, although I shall be glad to contribute."

"My manager, Joe Berman, will call upon you, and bring you my warm thanks."

He clasped the thin, dry old hand and closed the door upon his guest. It opened immediately upon Berman.

"What did he say? Will he help?"

"He will help. You'll go and see him."

"Right away?"

"Not today, not tomorrow," he said firmly. "Everything must wait for a few days. Leave me alone for a few minutes, will you, Joe?"

Berman looked at him earnestly, his eyes narrowed. "You didn't tell her, did you? No, don't tell me. I don't want to know. I'll see that no one comes in." His voice sank to a whisper as he went out and closed the door.

In the quiet room he sat behind his desk, alone at last, head bowed, jaw set, his hands clenched into fists on the writing pad. He must get this straight. Until he knew what he ought to do about the boy—not what he wanted to do, but what he ought to do—how could he go on with this campaign? It wasn't fair to shift the decision to Laura's will or wish. It was he who must decide and let her follow or refuse to follow. She could decide for herself but not for him. With resolution he unlocked his briefcase, searched among the papers, and found the gray envelope. Now, feeling for the thin sheet inside, he found what he had not seen before, a small photograph. The boy's face gazed at him, a gaunt young face, the neck too slender, the ears too big. Yet he recognized some ghost of himself, all but the eyes. The eyes were Asian.

He felt his own eyes suddenly hot and realized that tears were burning there. His son! He had dreamed of a son as every man dreams, but not one like this—not with a face like this! His throat tightened and his heart cried out against this son of his, born of an alien woman.

"Laura," he muttered, and reached for the telephone. He had put in a direct line between his desk and hers in the library at home where she worked, and now he dialed it, waiting, his heart beating.

"Is it you, Chris?"

"Yes, Laura, I want to tell you—"

He wanted to tell her—what? He found that he could not speak. His voice faded, he felt faint, breathless.

"Chris!" she called.

When he did not answer she cried out, "Are you all right, Chris? Shall I come?"

He pulled himself together. No, he did not want her pity. "Just a minute," he said, his voice breaking. He cleared his throat. "I don't know what was the matter. I suddenly couldn't—I just had to call you, darling. There's a picture here."

"A picture?"

"I didn't see it last night. I'm by myself for the moment. I decided I ought to read the letter. When I was about to take it out, a very small photograph—I suppose it was stuck in the bottom of the envelope before—"

"A photograph of—of the woman?"

"No, no, the boy! It sort of—gets me."

Hers was the silence now, a long silence during which he waited, endlessly, it seemed. His was the turn now to cry out whether she was all right, but he did not. He waited until at last her voice came to his ear.

"I'm coming, Chris. Meet me downstairs in the lobby? Let's go somewhere. Seashore, perhaps? I'll bring the car. Can you put people off?"

"I will," he said.

And so he had done. Ruthlessly he told Berman that he was gone for the day, told the office that something had come up, he couldn't explain—yes, a crisis, call it that—he tossed words over his shoulder, his secretary following him to the elevator. "But, Mr. Winters—"

"Tomorrow, tomorrow," he called back and leaped into the elevator.

He felt in his pocket. Yes, letter and photograph were there. He wanted them there, for the time had come to examine them both, and with Laura. Underneath everything he was slowly making up his mind, or his mind was making up itself. He must go to Korea and see this boy for himself, see how he was faring and why he was so thin. Never mind about Soonya! Laura must simply understand that it was the boy for whom he was responsible. Yes,

Laura, I am responsible for him. I should have known. I should never have taken the risk. I take it now, late, but not too late. He kept saying such words to her over and over inside himself while he waited in the lobby, and then, finally impatient, outside on the street in the brisk fresh wind of early spring. The day was glorious, but he had not seen it until now, the sky blue with floating white clouds, the air pure.

Then he saw her. She was in her own small car, the one he had bought for her birthday, dark green as a foil for her red-gold coloring, and she wore a gray suit with gloves but no hat, her hair coiled and the small curls loose and flying about her face. She was pale and he guessed that she had been crying, but he could not be sure, for she was composed, her eyes fearlessly meeting his.

He got in. "Want me to drive?"

"Yes, please," she said, somewhat to his surprise, for she liked to drive. Now, yielding, she curled down into the seat beside him, and thus, side by side, they drove through the city streets out to the boulevard and thence to the highway that led to the sea. Neither spoke. Twice or thrice he turned to smile at her and she smiled back and he was eased. She had been thinking, too, and perhaps in solitary thought they had come closer to understanding and accord than might have been possible had they remained in each other's company.

"I want you to know," he said suddenly, when they were in the open country, "I want you to know that whatever I decide, you are free to decide for yourself what you want to do."

"I shan't decide," she replied. "I've come that far, anyway. This has to be a decision for all of us—the four of us—the boy and his mother, you and I. It has to be right for everyone."

"You first," he said.

"No firsts," she replied.

Silence again until she spoke, after miles. "Did you bring the picture? May I see it?"

He nodded. "In my pocket. Get it out if you want to." And then he felt her hand rummaging at his side. She found it and he knew that she was studying it, with what thoughts he could not know.

"He looks terribly like you," she said at last. "I'd know him anywhere. If I saw him on the streets of Korea and hadn't the faintest inkling, I'd know. All except the eyes. Are they like—hers?"

"I don't remember," he was about to say, and then did not. No lies of any sort, he told himself, not the smallest!

"She had rather lovely eyes, dark, of course. All Koreans have dark eyes."

"I wonder," she said trying to be casual, "why it is that they all are of a color—not like us."

"I suppose because they have lived so long together on the same piece of land, with no mixtures. Give us their four thousand years on this piece of land we call ours and we'll all be the same color, too."

"Of course. I hadn't thought of that."

"Want to put the picture back?" he suggested after a moment.

"I'll hold it awhile," she said.

Silence again, and out of the corner of his eye he saw her studying the picture. After a few minutes she put it back into his pocket without speaking. At last he could not bear her silence—those silences, stretching into time until now on the horizon he could see the rim of the ocean. A smell of salt and marsh permeated the air.

"Shall we go to our cove?" he asked.

The cove was a beach, semicircling a narrow inlet and sheltered by dunes. At this time of year there would be no one in sight. They could stretch out on the sand and rest awhile first and soak in the noonday sun.

"Did you bring anything to eat?" he asked.

"I thought we'd stop for lunch at the Oyster House, and talk afterwards," she said.

"Right," he agreed. He swung into the fishing village and pulled up before the inn she had mentioned. They got out and walked side by side to the inn, not hand in hand as usual, but she with her hand in the curve of his elbow, not quite like a stranger, and yet in a sense they were strangers, and both knew it, not angry strangers, but two who must somehow be brought close again, and knowing it desirable and necessary and therefore inevitable, could be patient.

"Chris, there's a difference between us," she said.

They were on the beach of the cove now, the purple-black sea rolling in and the white gulls circling in the sunshine. He had been talking most of the time since they left the inn, at first with difficulty but now easily, or so he thought. She was beginning to understand, or so he thought. She lay on the sand, her head pillowed on his coat, and she turned and leaned her head on her elbow. The sun shone into her dark eyes and glinted on the fringes of her long dark-gold lashes, curling upward. Beneath the whiteness of her skin he discerned the shadows of childhood freckles which he had never seen before.

"What difference?" he inquired.

"You keep talking about the boy. I keep thinking about the woman."

"She doesn't matter."

"She matters to me. She matters terribly. I want to know her."

"But why? I've forgotten her."

"Ah, I know you better than that! If you'd been some oaf, some ordinary stupid boy, I'd believe you. But you're Chris, the man I love and respect." She turned over on her back and gazed up into the sky. "Oh, I had a hard time finding you! I was so determined not to make the mistake my mother made. She's the one who gave me my brains—not my father! I saw her fade into such a bleak old age, without companionship. I used to read about Madame Curie and wish that my mother could have had the happiness she had, married to a man who knew what she was talking about. And I vowed I'd never marry a man who didn't know what I was talking about. That's why I deluged you with my own work when you came back from Korea. And you were never bored. I'd have known if you'd been bored."

"Of course I wasn't bored. How could I be? You were telling me things I never knew, had never thought about, and looking all the time like a—like a—a—a Romney painting, only modern."

"My mother used to say that men didn't like intelligent women. She excused my father, but I hated him . . . Chris!"

"Yes?"

"Would you have married me if I'd been only pretty?"

"No."

"Or not pretty at all?"

He hesitated, then spoke. "I can't imagine that."

"What made you want to marry me?"

"I fell in love with you tentatively, that day you were the tall beautiful model wearing a white suit and a big white hat."

"But if I'd been—not intelligent?"

"I'd have forgotten you. Lots of pretty girls in the world! No, no, darling, if it interests you at this late date, it was the fascinating fact that you were a model on Tuesdays and Thursdays and the rest of the week were working at your oceanography stuff—"

"In which you were never interested before—"

"That's not the point. You were not interested in politics before. We've opened doors for each other. That's exciting. It gets more exciting every day. I don't want a wife who only knows how to wear clothes. Fact is, since we're being truthful in our privacy here, I like a wife who knows how to wear nothing at all—and when. And I like a wife who in the midst of love-making can use her magnificent brain to understand without words just how necessary tenderness is, and understanding, and sharing."

He leaned over her and looked down on her face, his hands in her hair. "Is it possible that you don't know how I love you?"

She looked up at him with eyes honest and direct. "Then how could you love Soonya?"

His hands fell, but she caught them and held them at her breast. "No, you must explain to me. I want to know, not because I mind—for I do mind so much that I wonder if my heart is broken—but not because I mind. I want to know—I must know what there is that you have never given me. Oh, that's not what I want to say—it's not what I mean . . . I'll try again."

She put his hands aside, sat up, and leaned her forehead on her hunched knees. She thought for a long moment and then lifted her head. "There was something in her that attracted you, which I don't have. What was it? Perhaps I have it and don't know it. What did she give you, something that I can't? No, don't mistake me—this isn't jealousy. It's humility. I would ask her if I could. Humbly I'd ask her."

She paused and looked at him with surprise dawning in her gaze. "If I could? But of course I can! There's no reason why I shouldn't go there and ask her."

"Oh, nonsense, Laura!"

The impatient cry escaped him and he checked himself. "Listen, darling, she wouldn't know what you're talking about. Matter of fact, I don't know either! Besides, I should be the one to go. I'm the culprit, not you! I want to see what the boy's situation is. If he's not getting an education, I'll put him in a boarding school."

"Not asking her anything? But it's her child. She's the mother!"

"You aren't defending her, are you? That's funny!"

"It may be funny to you, but not to me. You've not seen the boy since he was a few weeks old, and now you talk about putting him in boarding school! He's all she has."

"I'm not sure about that."

"What do you mean?"

"Probably been other men."

"And you say that—about a girl whom you—"

"Good God, Laura, the tide's coming in. We'll be caught!"

The tide had turned indeed, and the waves were rolling in upon the narrow beach. They seized their coats, and clasping hands, they ran around the rocky cliff which in a few minutes would have walled them in. Breathless and still hand in hand, they threw themselves down on the upper beach. A few people were walking in the distance, and at their feet the sandpipers raced down to the ocean and back again as the waves roared in and out.

"Where were we?" he gasped.

"Nowhere," she retorted. "Arguing about going to Korea—you to see the boy—of course I shall see him, too, but—"

He released her hand to light his pipe. "Laura, are you determined to go with me?"

She looked at him, imploring. "No, not if you say I must not. But I would like to go *alone*."

"Why?"

"Because you don't answer my question."

"I don't know how to answer it. If it's not enough that I was a lonely kid, that Korea was hell so far as I was concerned, and that I snatched at any small comfort available. Yes, I know we were married, but I didn't know if I'd live to see you again. For that matter, I didn't know what love really was—or can be—a boy can't know that, and all the time his senses are pounding at him."

"I don't believe you were ever an average, ordinary boy. All the time that you were in Korea, I was thinking of you, wondering if you were what I dreamed you were."

"You never let me know you were dreaming."

"Of course not. I didn't know if it would ever be more than dreaming. What if you were killed? But I didn't—do what you did."

He sighed. "Well, darling, I don't want to fall back on the old cliché that men and women, ergo boys and girls, are not the same where sex is concerned, for I have every evidence to the contrary. You're my perfect lover."

"Different from her?"

"Yes."

"How?"

"Infinitely different, infinitely better, infinitely satisfying."

"But how?"

He threw out his hands helplessly. "This isn't like you, Laura. You never press me."

She agreed, surprisingly, instantly. "It's not like me and it's not fair. So I am going to Korea, alone. I'll arrange to have the boy put into a boarding school. He's your son, and he must have everything he needs. As for her, I'll have to see. Perhaps nothing!"

"Laura, is this a quarrel?"

He put the question as a demand. She looked at him without anger but with a controlled determination.

"I want to go," she repeated. "I want to go soon—and alone."

II

SHE LEANED CLOSE to the window of the jet to catch the last glimpse of Chris. He stood on the upper deck of the airport, waving his brown scarf. He must have raced up the stairs to reach that point from which he could see her take off. Never had she spent three such days, so close to him and yet so far from him. Without the least doubt of their love, knowing that nothing could separate them, each invincibly sure of the other's loyalty, nevertheless they had not been able to communicate. She had debated the night before with herself. Should she or should she not go to his room if he did not come to hers? How long would she be gone, and would the fact that their last night had been spent apart assume monstrous meaning during the days that must pass before she could return? For she told herself that it was only a matter of days.

"Nevertheless, I'll feel relieved when you're safely back," he had said. "Consider my feelings," he had added. "Yield the point since I've yielded on your going alone, leaving me God knows to what. I shan't eat or sleep until you're home. It's like cutting myself in half. I don't even know what Korea itself is like now!"

Floating above Earth, she reviewed the past days. She had lived them in numbness. The house she had left to Greta, concentrating upon her work, aware that work was an escape. That was the way men escaped, too, into work. It was amazing how much suffering one could tolerate if there was work to do. She had finished her chapter on the benefits that ocean plants and animals are now known to hold for mankind: the electric eel, for example, providing an antidote to nerve gas; sea urchins, those small and delicate monsters, mapping the activity of white blood cells in their protective work against infection; the Portuguese man-of-war jelly fish through its stings helping to explain allergies. Her disciplined mind had found its own relief, a blessed relief, for without it, she, deeply emotional, could not have endured her own capacity for feeling.

The great jet aircraft trembled under the power of its own engines and lifted itself higher into space. She leaned back and closed her eyes. She was speeding into a world new to her. With Europe she was well acquainted but Asia was strange to her. She had not been curious about Korea even when Chris came home, so glad she was to have the separation over. And of course she had not dreamed that—

She opened her eyes as the jet leveled off. Never in her life had she felt so alone. Had it been wise, after all, to insist that she be the one to face the past? Was it jealousy that made the thought of a meeting between Chris and Soonya intolerable to her? Perhaps, perhaps, and she must know for herself exactly who Soonya was, see for herself the full measure of Soonya's charm and power. For she did not believe for a moment that Chris could have been attracted even superficially to an average girl, an ordinary girl, a cheap girl, even a girl with a plain face. He was subtle and fastidious and complex, and she delighted in those manifold aspects of his nature. The child—yes, of course, there was the child, but she must see the woman first and analyze for herself, as coolly as she had ever analyzed a specimen drawn from the depths of the sea, what this human being was, this female, who had shared with Chris his first real mating.

Her memory returned to her own wedding night. She had been a virgin, and she had not asked if he were virgin, too. She had wondered and then had been too shy, too proud, even to ask, and too innocent. Now, knowing what had taken place in that hut, that hooch, as Chris called it, she realized she should have known, the first night after he had come home, that there had been someone like Soonya. He was sure and knowing as he had not been before. He had been through it all—no, not all, for he had not loved Soonya as he loved her. No, and Soonya did not, could not, love him as she herself loved him. Soonya, an ignorant Korean girl . . .

"What did she do?" she had asked Chris yesterday.

They were in the living room sipping cocktails. He had come home early, and the late sunshine fell in golden bars through the tall narrow windows of the old house.

He had blushed, surprisingly. She had never seen him blush before. "What do you mean?" he countered.

"I mean, was she a teacher or a nurse or something?"

"Oh, no. I don't think she had a profession. She had been to school and she had a lovely voice. She used to sing,

I remember, but Koreans are always singing. They're a musical people, as I remember, although I don't think I really knew many others."

She had said no more, dreading to hear him speak of Soonya. Now she strove to put out of her mind the memories of her wedding night, but they were there, stored away in scenes she could not forget. The wedding had been beautiful, a simple ceremony in the great old church on Park Avenue where she had been christened. But her gown had been from the Paris of her grandmother's day, the satin name tag still bore the embroidered name of Worth, and she wore the real lace veil her grandmother had worn. And she had felt so gay, and Chris had, too, and they had held hands and almost danced down the aisle when the joyful music released them after the brief ceremony. It had been fun as well as a solemn rite, and she had enjoyed the reception at her parents' home and throwing the bouquet of lilies from the curving stairway, and then going to New England. She had said from the time she was twelve that her honeymoon must be in New England, in the ancient house where New England relatives still lived, and old uncle and aunt, who had been sweet and had left them alone all day until dinner. She and Chris had wandered the lanes and the meadows and she had moved in a dream of happiness. Everything was first for them, she had thought, they the first and only with each other, everything, everything, only now, of course, she knew she had not been the only one for him. The question was—

She avoided the question again. It was quite possible

that what he had told her was true. For last night when they had not lain close, she had mustered her courage.

"Chris, I don't know why I feel so cold. I can scarcely keep from shivering."

"Let me hold you."

She had let him hold her, and then suddenly he had moved away from her. "Are you changed?" he had asked. That was what he asked. "Are you changed?"

"No, not really," she had said. "Just sort of stunned. I feel as if I had been ill—weak and listless—not quite able to care about anything—yet, that is. A queer feeling . . . I daresay it won't last. It's just shock, I suppose."

She tried to laugh. "It's like coming up from the bottom of the ocean too quickly. Suddenly one just can't move or breathe."

"I'm sorry," he said. His voice was low and stricken.

Afterward, when he had gone away she had wondered, and wondered again now, whether she was changed. She argued with herself. It is not I who am changed. It is simply everything else that has changed. For if Chris is not what I thought he was, of course everything is changed. I am thrust into a world I do not know.

Bits and shreds of memory drifted through her mind. Her mother, the night before she was married, had said to her, "I hope you don't love Chris too much, darling."

She had opened her eyes wide at her mother. "How can I love him too much when he is to be my husband?"

"For your own good, I mean," her mother had explained, only at the time it had seemed inexplicable, and she had had no idea of what her mother meant.

"It makes me happy to love him all I can," she had said.

"That's dangerous," her mother had sighed. "It will break your heart someday."

Now she understood. She had loved Chris with the singleness of mind and heart that she applied to her work, her life, her self. There had been no room for casual friendships, for woman talk and idle pastimes. Childless, she had devoted her thought and time to Chris and work. Other women chattered about babies and housekeeping and husbands, and she had thought herself above them. Now she was humbled. She had no child, and it would have been better for her and for Chris if there had been a child. At least there would have been a child to divide her heart. Chris would not be there, alone and regnant.

She tried to imagine the child they might have had. She would have had to give up her work. No, that she could not imagine. Therefore, she could not imagine the child. She returned her thoughts to Chris. Those last few days, he had tried to be his natural self, and yet, as she very well knew, he was aware of her difference and wounded by it. At the last moment he had caught her to him. "I love only you, now and forever," and he had kissed her hard upon the lips.

She felt the kiss still burning there, and it occurred to her suddenly that Chris had changed no more than she. It was simply that she had not known the whole of him. All those years he had carried a secret in his memory, and though he had never told it to her, it had been there always, a part of him. Since she had loved what he had been could she not continue to love what he still was? To this question, which she pressed upon herself, she found no answer. For twenty-four hours she hung suspended in space, the great craft which contained her somehow symbolic of her own being. Earth was invisible under a floor of white clouds, parting now and again to show a glimpse of ocean beneath, its blue matching the sky above. The routine of life continued. She ate sparingly of food lavishly offered to her, she drank a cocktail or two, and a liqueur with her coffee after dinner. She slept fitfully when darkness fell and she woke at dawn. She washed and made up her pale face and brushed her hair. And all the time she was infinitely remote, the human beings caged with her mere automatons. She smiled in answer to a smile and replied with few words to strangers' greetings and remarks. She was nowhere, she was nothing, she was no one. She had neither past nor future, her past built upon a dream, her future unknown. What if she simply never went home again? What if she disappeared? No, she had a path planned, and she must follow it to its end.

She descended in Seoul, Korea, among people all of one color, hair dark, eyes dark. Around her a language she had never heard rose and fell in waves of strange sound. She had her directions, Chris had seen to that. The name of the hotel, the street, how she was to get there after customs.

It was a relief to hear that the young customs officer spoke English.

"How long you are staying, madame?"

"I don't know."

"Two weeks?"

"I hope not longer."

"More, you must get permission."

"I think it will not be more." He smiled at her, his teeth very white and even. "There is much beautiful here. I hope you stay long."

She had not smiled for days, but now she smiled. He was not quite a stranger when he smiled.

"Thank you," she said.

It was not difficult, after all, if she denied herself panic. Above all, she must be calm. She chose a cab which was, as she observed, an old jeep, its sides and roof made of tin cans pounded flat and nailed together, but it was a vehicle, and the driver, a young man in a patched cotton suit, washed to a faded gray, was cheerful, though without speaking English. He recognized the name of the hotel, and while the ride there was longer than it should have been, she suspected, she arrived. The jeep stopped with a jerk, the driver sprang from his seat, hauled out her two bags, and shouted. A porter ran out of the hotel, seized the bags, and waited while she counted the taxi fare, the driver helpful in pointing out the suitable coins with his crooked little finger. Again with the flashing white-toothed smile, he hurled the jeep into the crowded street, and she went into the hotel.

Chris had anticipated her. A cable was at the desk, and the clerk knew her name.

"Flowers in your room, madame," he said.

Flowers could only mean Chris again, and clutching the

cable in the envelope in her hand she followed a sprightly bellboy to her room. Yes, there were flowers, a tight bouquet of mixed colors, without fragrance. She paid off the boy, locked the door and opened the cable.

"I am there with you," Chris told her. "Night and day I am with you. I love you."

Suddenly she began to weep softly, she who never wept, and tears drained away the ache in her heart. Chris loved her—Chris was thinking of her. In a strange land, she was no longer alone. Distant though she was, she could see her home and Chris sitting, perhaps at his desk, lonely because she was not there. O precious home, let it never be destroyed through the weakness of the human beings it sheltered! She must be patient—she must forgive—forgive, because not to forgive is intolerable, and she must forgive lest she be homeless. For homeless was to be alone indeed, and to be alone was to be lost.

She was wakened by the light of dawn rising behind a mountain. Last night she had seen only city streets, but now, getting out of bed and going to the window, she saw the city, a medley of modern buildings and old houses, clustering in a bowl of valleys between mountains. They were not the forested mountains of home. These were great bare spines of rock, purple-shadowed at their base, but on their crests the light was golden. Spectacular beauty, and yet it was up those steep flanks that Chris had struggled as a young soldier, desperate with fatigue and homesickness, and never knowing why he was embattled. Pity trembled in her heart. He had described to her those bitter hours, he had shared with her, she had thought, his every mood during the years of their marriage. But he had not told her of Soonya until the letter came. Her heart hardened again.

An hour later she descended a broad stairway and crossed the lobby to the dining room for breakfast. The room was crowded with Americans and a few Korean men in Western dress. She hesitated at the door, searching for a place for herself, and saw only one empty chair, at a table for two, near the window which looked out upon a garden. The man at this table was Korean, a tall man of middle age, his pale handsome face grave. A waiter approached her.

"Sorry," he said. "No place just now."

She nodded toward the empty seat. "May I perhaps sit there?"

The waiter hesitated, then went to the Korean and spoke. The man looked up, surprised, saw her, and rose to his feet.

"Please," he said as she drew near.

"Thank you," she said, and took her seat.

She ordered her breakfast and then sat waiting, her head turned away, her gaze fixed upon the garden. It was a rock garden, and between the rocks were expanses of white sand, brushed smooth and then raked in spirals and circles. Small plants bloomed in the hollows of the rocks, and a crooked tree leaned over a pool. And all the time she was conscious of the tall distinguished figure across the table, but she did not speak. Then she heard his voice. His English was excellent.

"May I introduce myself?"

He took out his wallet, extracted a card and put it on the table before her. She read his name aloud. "Mr. Choe Yu-ren?"

"Businessman," he said, smiling. "I am in pharmaceutics. My own firm."

She looked up and met his kindly gaze. "Good morning, Mr. Choe."

He bowed. "You are traveling alone, madame?"

"Yes, on personal business."

"Staying some time, perhaps?"

"I hope not. Ah, don't misunderstand me! It is simply that I am anxious to get home, for personal reasons again, and I have no time to sightsee, I am sorry to say. I shall be here only a few days, perhaps."

She was aware of his atmosphere, a pleasant warmth combined with an air of worldly wisdom. He put down his fork—a very American breakfast, she thought, ham and eggs, toast and coffee, an empty fruit dish.

"Forgive me," he said. "I am not prying, I hope. It is merely that I spent very happy years in your country as a student—Yale, 1935—and now I go back each year for business contracts. My firm has connections with leading pharmaceutical companies in your country, and I always enjoy my visits. Your people are extraordinarily hospitable."

He hesitated and continued. "Is this your first visit to Korea?"

"Yes," she said.

He hesitated again and she was aware of his fine dark

eyes, questioning. She made no reply. The waiter brought her sliced orange and coffee, boiled egg and toast. When he had gone the man spoke again.

"Forgive me if I presume, but it is seldom that I have the chance to return the kindness I have met in your country. If there is anything I can do to help you here, I pray you will accept my help. I wish I could introduce my wife, but, alas, she died last year, and I live here alone in the hotel except on weekends, when I return to my house in the country, where my mother lives. My son is in college at my own alma mater in your country, and I have no other children."

She found herself looking at him, listening to him, thinking that she had never found a more beautiful human being, merely to see. He was tall, and his Western suit of dark gray cloth was of English cut. His hair, turning white at the temples, was dark, and his eyes were a dark brown. Except for the shape of those eyes, he might have passed for Italian, or perhaps Spanish, but the eyes were Asian. His bearing, his frankness, inspired trust, and upon impulse she opened her handbag and took out the small card upon which Chris had written Soonya's address.

"Can you tell me where this is, please?"

He studied the card and became grave again. "It is a very difficult place to find, quite far from here at the southern edge of the city. How are you going? By car, of course?"

"I thought of a cab."

"But surely you are not going alone?"

"I don't know anyone here."

He pondered. "Perhaps someone at your American Embassy?"

"Oh, no," she said quickly. "My business is quite private."

He returned the card to her and she replaced it in her bag. He was silent, considering, as he finished his eggs and drank his coffee. Then he pushed the dishes aside.

"Will you let me go with you?" he asked abruptly.

She was startled. "Oh, I couldn't. You are busy."

"I am master of my own time and I have only to make a telephone call to my office. Believe me, I cannot allow an American lady to go to that part of our city alone. If you prefer, I will summon my secretary to go with us. Yes, it occurs to me that you do not know me."

"It's not that," she said, and could not go on.

"You wish also to remain private?" he suggested. "In that case I can wait in the taxi while you—"

She was embarrassed. "It is not my business, actually. It is something that concerns my husband."

"You are married, then."

"Yes, Mrs. Winters—Christopher Winters."

"From—"

"Philadelphia."

He smiled, and his somewhat stern face warmed with characteristic suddenness. "Ah, Philadelphia! I know that beautiful city. I spent my Christmas holidays there with Dr. Harmsworth and his wife. Do you know him?"

"The great Orientalist?"

"Ah, you do know him!"

"We've only met."

"Then you remember him, for he cannot be forgotten once he is seen. I call him my American father. Now he is very old, of course, but I go to see him when I am in your country. He calls me his Korean son. And my own son continues the tradition while he is in college in America, too, and spends his holidays there in that beautiful old house. Alas, the mistress no longer lives. Mrs. Harmsworth died while I was in graduate school."

Suddenly she trusted him and in the decision she felt safe—yes, and comforted. She had a friend here.

"Please do come with me," she said quietly.

"As soon as your breakfast is eaten," he replied.

She decided during that journey through the streets of Seoul that she would make no explanations. Long ago, as a child, she had learned never to explain, not herself, not her actions. When her mother accused her, scolded her, she replied always by silence. To ask for no explanation, to give none in return, had provided an atmosphere of peace in her youth, her marriage, her home. Now as she rode through crowded streets and parks she said little and Mr. Choe was too courteous, too well bred, to ask questions. Instead he explained the monuments they passed, he expressed the hope now that she would have time to visit the palaces of the kings now dead, he offered to accompany her to the new museum someday before she returned to her own country.

She smiled, she hoped that this would all be possible, she admired in private his handsome profile. She was accustomed to men, for as a scientist she worked among them, but this was a man new to her, and in more than appearance. He had the polish of old ivory, smooth and opaque, solid yet precious—very complex, she decided, and difficult to comprehend. Her impulse had been to trust and was now to doubt. With the patience she had learned from her training in long hours of work in her laboratory, she observed this man. He was masculine and yet there was a feline grace. He was direct and without shyness, and yet she was aware of much unsaid as he talked. She became aware, too, of his skilful questions.

"You are an artist, Mrs. Winters?"

"No. Why do you think so?"

"You have an air, a style, detached and yet comprehending."

"I am a scientist."

He was immensely interested. "A woman and a scientist? Is this not a contradiction?"

"Not in my country, though not usual, I admit. I am an oceanographer—like you, a pharmacologist only a marine one!"

"And you make ocean expeditions in search of material for medical use? We Koreans also use sea materials for healing."

"Yes, sometimes I go on expeditions. Not quite as often as I used to do, before my marriage."

"For example, what expedition?"

"Well, the last one was off the coast of Panama. I wanted to collect plankton."

"You were not alone, surely?"

"No, three other scientists were with me. We were studying the ocean itself—the bottom, its shapes and contours, the sea water, its chemistry and physics, currents, plant life, animal life—everything possible. Each of us had a responsibility. Mine was—is—to study that type of life which hovers between plant and animal, and may be either, or both."

"Ah, the bridge creatures! Yes, they are important—but you amaze me!"

She did not answer, for they had stopped at a small brick house, crowded between two larger ones. He spoke to the cab driver, who nodded.

"We have arrived, Mrs. Winters," Mr. Choe said. "If you will allow me, I will introduce you, and then wait for you outside the house."

Now that the moment of meeting had come, she could not face it alone. "Please come with me. I shan't be able to understand what is said. I will tell you. I have come to find a child, and his mother."

"In that case," Mr. Choe said.

He descended from the cab and motioned to the driver with his large elegant hand that he was to wait.

"Now, Mrs. Winters," he went on, "allow me to precede you. I will inquire. What is the name, please?"

"Miss—Mrs.—Kim—and the first name is Soonya."

He received this with blank looks, conveying his determination to show neither concern nor curiosity, and knocking on the half-open wooden door, he coughed loudly. An old woman in a patched black cotton skirt and green bodice pulled the door wide. He spoke, and she nodded. He spoke again, and she shook her head. He turned.

"Mrs. Winters, Miss Kim is sleeping. She works at night

in a—she works at night and wakes late. This is her mother. She invites you to come in. She will rouse her daughter."

She considered and then faced her own reluctance. "Is there also a child here?"

He asked the old woman and she replied. He translated. "There is a child."

"A boy?"

"A boy."

"Is he here now?"

He put the question and the old woman shook her head and burst into loud angry talk. He put up his hand to silence her and translated.

"He is not here at this moment. She says the boy is much trouble. He runs away and she does not know where he is until he comes home hungry. She complains that she and the mother do not know what to do with him. He is a wild boy, aged eleven."

"I will come in," she said. "I wish to see the mother and talk with her. I am sorry to have her waked, if she is tired, but I have come a long way, and I want to go home as soon as possible."

"I understand," he said gravely.

They went into a small cramped room, the floor of tamped earth, varnished or polished, she did not know which, but very clean. A low table, a few books, floor cushions, and on one wall a landscape scroll, and there was no other furniture. The old woman patted a cushion.

"She invites you to be seated," Mr. Choe said.

They seated themselves and the woman disappeared.

They waited, Mr. Choe now silent, and she pondered the necessity, or the wisdom, of explaining to him why she was here, then once more decided against explanation. A few hours ago she had never seen this man and might never see him again after today, now that he had served the purpose of bringing her to this house. She looked across at him and smiled, gravely, gratefully. He began an apology.

"This house is quite poor. I don't know what Miss Kim does for a living. Perhaps she is married, in which case I can imagine her husband is perhaps a clerk in a store, or in the post office or something like that. I doubt he is a teacher, unless in an elementary school. She helps in a bar or something like that, perhaps. Most of the bar girls are married and work at night when the husband can be at home. Of course in this case she is caring for her old mother, and perhaps the husband too works at night, since it is difficult to live."

She made no reply to this and indeed could not, for now the inner door opened softly and Soonya stood there in the doorway. She recognized her instantly, for this woman, though no longer young, was in her full bloom. She wore Korean dress, a long dark skirt and a white bodice crossed at the bosom. Her dark hair was coiled on the back of her head and her dark eyes, set in the pale cream face and beneath flying dark eyebrows, were tender and questioning. It was so gentle a face, and the whole woman so feminine in grace, small and fine of bone, yet rounded in contours, that try as she would, Laura could not immediately dislike her. She was prone to first impressions, liking or disliking, and she had consciously decided that she would base her decisions upon the emotion of this moment. Nor had she hid from herself her private wish to dislike Soonya.

"I will not concern myself with the woman," she had told Chris. "I owe her nothing. But the boy, because he is yours—yes, I want to see that he gets an education. Not here, Chris, but in his own country."

Chris had looked at her blankly. "I suppose it *is* his country. Strange to think of that!"

Soonya came in, her feet noiseless in small rubber slippers, the toes slightly upturned. She paused in front of Mr. Choe and poured out a stream of talk in a soft high voice, almost a child's voice. Mr. Choe listened with growing astonishment, his lips pursed.

"What is she saying?" Laura asked at last.

"She has seen me before," Mr. Choe said without explanation.

Laura waited, and when he did not speak she put another question. "Ought I to know more?"

"No," Mr. Choe said firmly. "I remember now who she is."

She hesitated, feeling strangely blocked and even ignored. For Mr. Choe motioned to Soonya to be seated and they continued their conversation, he with a question now and again, and she with her urgent, soft, rushing talk. The old woman came in and sat, crouched against the inner wall. At the door stray children gathered, pushing each other this way and that in order to see better what was going on. Mr. Choe looked up, frowned at them and then shouted at them. They ran into the street and then imperceptibly, as talk continued, they crept near again.

Laura waited, hours it seemed, but perhaps only half an hour, and Mr. Choe apologized.

"Excuse me, please," he said. "She is in trouble with the landlord. Her son is hard to manage and the landlord wishes her to move away. It seems the boy steals something now and then from the neighbors. Also, she has no husband. She supports herself and the mother and son."

"Where does she work?" Laura asked.

Mr. Choe showed embarrassment. He took out a large silk handkerchief and wiped his handsome brow and then the palms of his hands. "I will explain to you later," he said. "Meantime she has also told me her greatest difficulty." He paused and continued. "This child—he is not a usual boy. He is the son of an American man. Twelve years ago she met this man when he was here after the war. They shared a life together for a year and more. She hoped he would marry her and he promised to return to this country. He went to America when the child was a month old, and from then on she has heard nothing from him. Meantime she has had to care for the child alone, although it is not her duty to do so."

She heard this, her heart pounding. She would not betray Chris. Let them think she had come only as a friend, not as a wife.

"Certainly it is her duty," she said firmly. "She is the child's mother."

Mr. Choe looked at her steadily, his hands outspread on his knees. "Here it is the father who is responsible for the child. When there is no father, there is no family. The child is lost. He cannot go to school, nor can he hold a job, because the father has not registered his birth. So far as we are concerned, the child has not been born. He has no family, no one stands behind him. Therefore, he does not exist."

She felt a welcome and supporting rush of anger. "That is ridiculous. The child is here. He does exist."

"Not legally," Mr. Choe said.

She could not answer. She was in a strange world, a world she had not imagined, among a people she did not know. She turned to Soonya with a look that was almost pleading. Surely there was at least the bond of womanhood between them?

And Soonya, as though answering the look, rose and searched in a drawer in the low table that stood in the middle of the room. From a silk-wrapped envelope, she drew two photographs which she gave to Mr. Choe, murmuring explanations in her soft voice. He examined them and handed them to Laura. "The child's father."

She did not wish to look at those photographs and would have given half her life to have refused them now, but she took them, nevertheless. Yes, this was Chris, the young Chris with whom she had then already been in love, a wondering, questioning first love, quivering with joy, hiding itself in shyness and waiting. He stood in one photograph, with his arm about Soonya's shoulder, a very young Soonya, laughing up into his smiling face. And in the second he was holding his son in his arms, his baby son, and Soonya was leaning her head against his shoulder.

I'll never see him with my son in his arms, she thought, and controlling the strong thrust of pain in her heart she gave the pictures again to Soonya. Now she knew she must communicate with this woman.

"Do you still speak English?" she asked.

Soonya shook her head. "Too little I speak now."

Mr. Choe encouraged her. "Do not be shy. She is your friend. She has come to look for you."

Soonya touched her breast with a small delicate hand. "You look for me?"

"Yes," Laura said. "I have come a long, long way."

She broke off. How was she to continue except by the truth? She looked from one Asian face to the other. Puzzlement, polite but clear, courteous patience, a veiled curiosity, silent waiting. These were expressed in Asian eyes, in the pose of Asian hands. Soonya felt the teapot, found it hot, and filled the teabowls on the low table. Mr. Choe lifted his bowl and drank in loud sips. Soonya sat on the floor, her hands folded in her lap. Their eyes were upon Laura and they waited.

Now she, knowing the moment of revelation had come, opened her handbag and took out a thin leather booklet. She opened it upon the face of Chris, her Chris, the way he was now, the man who was her husband. She looked at the eyes—honest eyes? Oh, surely honest eyes! Without a word then, she handed the picture to Soonya.

Soonya took it, looked at it, looked at it again with more than interest, and lifted her eyes to Laura's face.

"He it is." Her voice was a whisper, but Laura heard and nodded. Soonya handed the booklet to Mr. Choe. He took it and examined the face.

"She says it is her child's father."

"I know that," Laura said quietly. She felt faint, the blood pounded through her head, her heart beat at twice its usual speed.

Mr. Choe turned to Soonya and asked a question in Korean.

"Chris-to-pha Winters-s," Soonya said, slowly and distinctly.

Mr. Choe closed the folder and gave it back to Laura. "Mrs. Winters," he said, "you are a brave and generous woman."

To her horror, tears rushed to her eyes and rolled down her cheeks. She felt for her handkerchief, could not find it. Mr. Choe gave her his silk handkerchief and she took it and wiped the tears away.

"I would like to talk with you alone," she told him. "Let us return to the car."

"Whatever you wish," he said, and spoke to Soonya. She listened, rose to her feet and then hesitated. Suddenly, as though making up her mind not to be afraid, she paused on her way and stopped beside Laura, as though to speak. But she did not speak. Instead, Laura felt upon her cheek the brush of a palm soft as a moth's wing.

He glanced at her as she sat beside him in the car, her gloved hands folded on her brown leather handbag resting on her lap. She had said not a word since they left the small house where Soonya lived, and now, catching his glance, she tried to smile and could not. They were alone, were they not, and still she could not say a word. The people in the crowded streets, the unfamiliar signs on shops, the stark mountains rising beyond the city, all were strange, and the tall man at her side was a stranger. Where could they go so that she might be alone with him? And would she, after all, confide in him? She had never been able to speak easily of inward feelings. A silent child, a silent woman, she had often felt herself a silent wife, expressing love through gesture and touch and act rather than through words. But this morning Chris was very far away. Here there was no one—no one except this man whom by barest chance she had met only this morning, and now clung to, perhaps merely because he spoke English.

"You are weary," he said. "I think we must have some tea and perhaps a little food. It is past noon. Would you—" He paused, lifting his fine eyebrows. "Why not? You are American, and I have visited in American homes. Will you come to my house and have food and tea? There we can talk. While my old mother speaks no English, she will be glad to see you. She thanks Americans for their kindness to me when I was young and far from home. And for this kindness now given to my son."

"I'd be grateful," she murmured.

The car sped through the streets, honking the horn, dividing the people as a prow of a ship divides the waves. Mr. Choe was well known, it seemed, for people spoke his name, and she heard it again and again through the open window. He sat very straight, ignoring them, and not speaking again until they had left the city and a road which ended in a peaceful lane, lined with poplars already in young green leaf. The lane ended at a wide wooden gate, painted red and set in a high gray brick wall. The driver shouted and the gate swung open slowly, an old man holding the bar.

"Here is my ancestral home," Mr. Choe said. He led Laura into a garden, large and quiet, which was surrounded, so far as she could see, by a vast one-story house, whose curving roof was upheld by huge vermilion pillars.

"A peaceful place," she observed.

"Not always," he replied. "It was occupied by a Japanese general during the many years of Japanese rule. When the Americans came, an American general lived here. It has only been in the last ten years that our property has been restored to us."

A maid was waiting at the entrance to remove their shoes and replace them with cloth slippers. Mr. Choe spoke to her in low tones, she nodded and disappeared, and he led the way into the house itself.

"The maid will announce us to my mother," he said, "and meanwhile we will rest. Do not hurry yourself. Be seated here where you can look into the garden and see the pool. It is the season when life springs again after the winter. Let this be a good omen for you."

The room was large and the furniture was Western, easy chairs and sofas, a grass-green carpet on the floor and curtains of gold satin at the windows. On one side was a shoji wall, but the shoji were closed and what was beyond she could not guess. She sank into one of the chairs, a comfortable resting place cushioned in gold satin. From here she could follow with her eyes a winding path of stepping stones across the lawn and ending in a pool fed by a waterfall at its farther end. Beyond it were more curving roofs.

Mr. Choe had seated himself and now he opened a black lacquer box with a plum-blossom design in mother-of-pearl and offered her a cigarette. When she refused with a slight shake of her head he lit one for himself. A maid brought in tea, pot and bowls, and was followed by a second maid with a tray of cakes and sweetmeats.

"Refresh yourself," Mr. Choe said. "Here you may rest. You are agitated and fatigued."

Silently they drank tea, and slowly she felt her tension ease. She put her bowl on the table by her chair, and Mr. Choe filled it with fresh tea. As he did so, they exchanged a look, hers questioning, his encouraging.

Thus encouraged she began somewhat abruptly. "Am I wrong in thinking you knew Soonya?"

"Everyone knows her," he replied. "Try this sweetmeat. It is made by a recipe of my mother's. We like it very much."

She took a small filled cake from the tray and tasted it.

"Delicious," she said, "but how is it that everyone knows Soonya?"

"She is famous for the house she keeps," he told her. "She is what you may call a madam, and yet she is not like any other. You saw the modest way in which she lives. I myself had never seen it before. I did not know she lived there. Nor did I know her by the name of Kim Soonya. Professionally she has another name. And her professional house, The House of Flowers, is famous for its richness and for its beautiful, well-bred girls. She trains them in all the arts. She is herself a singer and dancer, although she no longer practices these arts. She makes but one rule. She will have only Korean clients, and since her prices are high, they are all men of wealth."

She noticed that he did not say "we." Did this mean that he himself did not frequent The House of Flowers? Yet he knew Soonya. Ah, what concern was it of hers when she was here only because of Chris?

She began again, plunging into the tangle of feelings and facts. "My husband was here twelve years ago. He met Soonya then, when she was a very young girl. They had a son. All these years he did not tell me. We have been—we are—happily married. I suppose there was no reason why he should have told me, except that I had supposed we had no secrets from each other. And now the boy has written a letter saying that he has no chance to go to school. I am here to—"

Mr. Choe leaned forward. "My dear madame, are you telling me that your husband sent you here alone to—"

"I came of my own free will," she broke in. "It is a difficult moment for us. It was impossible for him to get away. Besides, the question of what to do about the boy concerns me, too. I don't want my husband's son to grow up ignorant, and—" She was incurably honest and she went on, though reluctantly. "I suppose I wanted to see for myself, too, how such a thing could have happened."

"What is more natural?" Mr. Choe said gently. "You love your husband. It is a wound to a woman's heart in any country when the husband takes another woman."

"We were only just married."

She looked at him and saw in his Asian eyes a depth of understanding, a compassion that was too much for her to endure. Her lip trembled and she tried to smile. "We are very happily married, you must know. Even this—this—experience seems not to have separated us. It sounds impossible, but each of us understands how the other one feels and we—each of us tries to—to mitigate, or share—"

"I do understand," he said gravely. "Yet the self is wounded and it alone can heal itself. So you came here first to see the woman, did you not, and then the boy? Well, what did you think of the woman?"

She pondered the question. "I scarcely know. Perhaps it's not thinking so much as feeling. She is soft and gentle."

"She is as hard as iron," Mr. Choe said.

"But she touched my cheek."

"Yes, she is also able to feel pity."

"Pity for me?"

"Pity for another woman. She has no illusions about men. You should hear her give a lecture to her girls."

He fell into a fit of silent laughter. "I know her well—oh, very well. I am, in fact one of her clients. She is quite famous, you know. She takes revenge on—well, let us say life—by allowing none but Korean men to enter her House of Flowers. No Western man, especially no American man, may enter her door. 'Let them go to the third-rate places where they belong.' This is her revenge. Korean men, if they can pay her price, are sure of meeting only girls who do not associate with the lower classes and foreigners. We know her girls are clean and well educated. Above all, we know they are Koreans."

She heard this with a tumult of feeling—indignation, and wonder—mingled with some amusement. Oh, poor Chris!

"Was she always like this?" she inquired.

"Always? Oh, no," Mr. Choe replied. "When I first met her—" he paused, coughed slightly.

"Please don't be shy!" she urged. "We've passed that, haven't we? Although we've known each other such a short while?"

He laughed. "You are very—ah—understanding. Well, when I first met her she did not have a place of her own. She was singing and dancing and so on, an entertainer primarily, in quite a decent, well-known house. I was attracted by the profound sadness which enveloped her, even when she was singing some foolish gay song or dancing. I invited her to have a drink with me, and we soon fell into talk—as you and I have—and she told me that she had an old mother and a son to support. Later I heard some of the story of the son, at least that his father was American and that she was still dreaming of how to get into communication with—ah—the American. She had written but there had been no reply." He smiled. "I remember being somewhat jealous and because it seemed to me obvious that she would never have a reply, I urged her to set up her own house. As a matter of fact, I lent her the money, which she has returned to me entirely. She is a good businesswoman."

She listened, marveling at the fate which had led her to this man, so strangely related to her and to Chris through Soonya, and before she could consider a question or reply to what he had said, the maid appeared at the door with a message.

"Ah," Mr. Choe said. "My mother is ready to receive us."

They followed the maid, and were ushered into a central room in the house. She knew it was central, for on four sides the shoji had been pushed back to give way to other rooms. There in the middle of a jeweled setting, the ondul floor gleaming, the floor cushions of crimson velvet and black satin, the low table, the low bookcases of shining black lacquer inlaid with mother-of-pearl, sat a small white-haired woman, her face exquisite even in age. In this pale wrinkled face, a cameo, two great black eyes burned as though they were young. Beneath them the mouth was grave.

Mr. Choe bowed and spoke to her in Korean. She nodded, still unsmiling, and stared at the visitor. Then in a high, soft voice, scarcely audible, she asked a question. Mr. Choe translated.

"My mother wishes to know if you have sons."

"I'm sorry, no," she replied.

The great eyes staring unblinking upon this news, the soft voice pronounced a few words more.

"My mother says that you are pretty, but she does not like the color of your hair and eyes."

Laura laughed. "Neither do I! I've always wanted to be dark. But what can I do? I must accept myself as I am."

This, translated, brought a small smile to the ivory face. The lady spoke a few words in a low voice.

Mr. Choe laughed in turn, then bowed as his mother

spoke again and turned to Laura. "We are dismissed," he said. "My mother is nearly ninety and she is easily impatient. We humor her, and we are very proud of her age. She is the darling of the household."

Laura too bowed, and Mr. Choe, first adjusting a shoji to prevent the breath of wind that was creeping in from the garden, led the way again to the front door, where the car waited.

"You are very weary after this long morning," Mr. Choe said. "Let us return to the hotel and meet again tomorrow? If I can be of service—"

She stepped into the car, he took his seat beside her, and in silence they drove the half hour to the city. She was indeed weary, so much had impinged upon mind and senses in this brief day, and she was glad of his silence. At the hotel he escorted her to the elevator, bowed formally, his face bland and inscrutable, and she went upstairs to her room. It was as she had left it except that on the table stood a small plum tree in a green pot. It was in full bloom, a shimmer of white in the afternoon sun streaming in from the window.

She looked at the card attached. It was from Mr. Choe. Somehow he had found a moment or perhaps he had only spoken to a maid in his house. At any rate, he had found the moment, remembering that she was alone, to send her a plum tree, the symbol of persistent life. Life? She had had a little too much of it today, she was tired, and she longed for escape. Were she at home, she would have escaped to her laboratory, or even, perhaps, to the cool green depths somewhere in an ocean. As it was, she undressed, lay down on her bed, and fell into deep and instant sleep.

It was morning of the next day when she woke. For a moment the rosy light from the window beguiled her into thinking that it was the sunset of the day before. But this light was unmistakably that of dawn. She rose, wondering at the lost and dreamless hours, then realized that she was feeling rested and refreshed and not in the least afraid anymore. She did not even feel haste. Instead she went back to bed for an hour, then bathed and dressed with an astonishing sense of leisure. It was still early, but she walked down the stairs and into the dining room, now empty except for three young men who were probably guests. Obviously it was too early for Mr. Choe, and she found herself rather glad this morning to be without him. She might even take a walk alone, and then come back and write a letter to Chris. After that—well, after that she would proceed to do whatever she felt was next.

No one came into the dining room while she finished her breakfast, and afterward she sauntered out to the street instead of returning to her room. People were already busy, clerks walking to offices, women going to market, children to school. The street was a mélange of old poverty and new prosperity, if indeed it was prosperity. Opposite the hotel entrance a flower garden marked the division between opposing streets, and she crossed to see what two old men were doing. They were city gardeners, obviously, and obviously, too, in argument over the small plants they were setting out. The younger produced a map to prove his point, for she glanced over his shoulder and saw a colored drawing of squares and stars designed for the flower bed, she supposed. She was mildly amused at this argument that might have happened in any country. Evidently the old man was convinced, though against his will, for he grunted, pulled up plants and began anew. And she, about to continue her walk, felt a tug at her jacket from behind, and turning, was faced with five or six ragged urchins, beggar children, who held out filthy small hands for coin.

"Never give to beggars," Chris had warned. "Especially, never to children who beg. Your life will be miserable."

She remembered and was about to escape when she saw a child who stood apart, a tiny girl, bone thin, whose age she could not guess. She paused, not heeding the clamor of the others. Now she put out her right hand and lifted the child's face and looked down into it. No Asian child, this! Yet the eyes were Asian in their almond shape, wide, lovely, yes, but not dark, in spite of all. They were hazel, glints of blue through the brown. And the child's hair was not black. Straight as it was, hanging in tangles, it was a light brown. And the child's bones, fleshless, were nevertheless of a sturdy structure, without the delicate finials of Asian hands and feet.

She stooped to bring her face close to this small, exquisite face, unwashed and listless in spite of beauty.

"Who are you?" she whispered, though knowing she could not be understood.

The other children had ceased their begging. Curious and eager, they pressed about the two, and perceiving that this child had some advantage, the largest of the children, a boy, took the little girl's hand and forced her to seem to beg. The little girl resisted, nevertheless. She would not beg, and suddenly seeking escape, she burrowed her way among the children and ran down the street before she could be caught.

"Oh, I've lost her," Laura cried, and pushing the children away, she ran after the little girl, now hidden in the alleyways behind the hotel. Nevertheless, she continued to pursue, and when she turned a corner, she saw the child again, this time in the distance, at a back entrance, she supposed, to the hotel. There the child was waiting as though for someone, and, fearing that she might again escape, Laura stood still behind a crooked tree that had forced its way between the hotel and the sidewalk. It was soon obvious that the child was indeed waiting, and suddenly it could be seen why she waited. For a servingman came out of the hotel with a bucket of refuse which he poured into a wooden box that stood outside the door. The child, seeing him come, had hidden herself behind a wall, but when the man was gone, she stole out from her hiding place, looking left and right and seeing no one, she fell upon the refuse, pushing it about with her little hands, searching and finding bits of food here and there which she thrust into her mouth.

What could she do? Laura asked herself. If she showed herself the child would run away. And even if she caught the child, what could she do to help her? There must be many such children—many, many! And she was here to find only one, and she had found him—at least, where he lived. Let her not involve herself with others. She came of prudent Boston stock. Better to take care of one's own first, and then—

Alas, the child had seen her! Snatching her handfuls she ran, fleet as a sandpiper, down a secret alley and was gone. And Laura, after waiting, could do nothing except return again to the street, but without heart now to continue her walk. Instead she entered the hotel, went to her room and wrote a letter to Chris.

It took time, that letter. The sun climbed slowly to the zenith before she had finished. Yet it was not a long letter, at that. It was only long in time of writing, for how to explain Mr. Choe to Chris, and how to express what she felt about Soonya, a feeling still so vague, the contrast between the soft hand on her cheek and Mr. Choe's insisting voice, "She is iron," and besides, she had not seen the boy. The letter did her good, nevertheless, for it expressed compactly even the vagueness of her feelings.

"It is too soon," she wrote, "but I have begun. I have seen Soonya but I have not talked to her. I must find the boy today if I can. It occurs to me that she may not want to give him up. I feel sorry for him living with that old grandmother. Soonya"—

She crossed the name out. No, she would not tell Chris yet about The House of Flowers. For that matter, she could do no more than mention Mr. Choe. Too much had happened yesterday, and too quickly. Nor did she tell him about the starving child. It was all too difficult. She wrote the three important words, "I love you," and sealed her letter.

Yes, now she must return to the house where Soonya lived, she must return alone, and establish her own communication; perhaps the boy would be there today. She had better go at once, for in the afternoon it was likely that Soonya would be busy at The House of Flowers. The sun was hot by now and she had better wear a hat. And at the moment when she was about to leave she noticed that the plum tree was wilting. She felt of the earth in the pot. It was dry, and putting down her bag she went to the bathroom, filled a glass with water and poured it on the roots.

It was not difficult to find Soonya's house again. She had a good sense of direction—it was always she, when Chris was driving, who studied the routes and read the maps. She had been able to direct the cab driver this morning, and in a much shorter time today than it had taken yesterday, or so she thought, she reached the small brick house again. Soonya met her. She had been about to leave on business of her own, but when the cab drew up and Laura emerged, she quietly set down her handbag and umbrella, and putting out her hand she drew her guest inside the house. No one else was there, the old mother not in sight, and no boy about.

She felt no ease in being alone with Soonya, and yet was sensible enough to realize that this might be good for them both, an undisturbed hour. But could Soonya speak enough English? Allowing no Americans in The House of Flowers, she might have had no opportunity to learn more English than she had once had, long ago. And yesterday she had not spoken more than a few words in English, trusting to Mr. Choe as translator. Laura followed Soonya to an inner room she had not seen yesterday, Soonya's bedroom, it seemed, a pleasantly furnished room, strangely American, with pink flowered curtains at the window, an enormous bed curtained with pink silk, and floor cushions covered in the same material. There was one picture on the dressing table, a photograph of Chris, and seeing that young face, a boy's face, smiling and self-confident, she fought a sudden impulse to weep. Had it been in this room?

Soonya, following her gaze, went to the table and turned the photograph face to the wall.

"Long time ago," she said in English. "Very long time ago. He is not the same man now. He is your husband. I have memory—nothing more."

"You have the child," Laura said.

Soonya threw her a quick glance from slanting eyes. "You take him away?"

"No," Laura said.

"Then why you are here?"

Laura shook her head. "I ask myself. But since the boy wrote to his—to my husband, it seemed only right that we should know whether it is true that he is in need, growing up without education."

Soonya put up a swift hand. "Not my mistake for this! He cannot go school because he cannot be registered. And children are laughing at him there. They call him dirty words. Because his father is American. He asks me, why is father American? How can I explain such difficulty? But anyway, he get some education. I have for him sometimes private teacher—you call tutor?"

She gazed at Soonya's softly flushed face. They were

sitting on the floor cushions, a low table between them. The shoji was open to a rock garden, and upon the branch of a crooked tree a small brown bird sang a sudden triad of notes, piercingly sweet. She turned her head to watch. The song was greater than the minuscule bird body, the throat swelling, the wings fluttering.

"And why is his father American?" she murmured.

A long instant passed before Soonya answered. "At first it is true I am not in love with him," she said at last. "I was very poor. After the war everyone is very poor. My father killed and house gone by bombing. I was only child. Many girls like me. So there is nothing we can do except to sing and dance and live with American man. At first I wish only sing and dance, not man."

"How old were you?"

The lovely eyes widened. "I am having only eighteen years—seventeen years by American count. But I am tall as now. Still I am afraid of man, all man. When some man looks at me I look aside. Then one night I see one man come in better than others."

"Better?"

"Yes, so tall, so beautiful, so sad. He is not laughing and yelling loudly like others, just quiet and sad. He is not looking at girls. Then one very noisy boy, hooligan from Texas maybe, and drinking, catch me, pull me away. Then I am crying loudly. Now tall sad man get up, and so quickly he tears me free and leads me to his table. I am already crying very much and he find handkerchiefs and give me."

But this was not what Chris had told her. He had not

sought her out, nor brought her to his table. Soonya was dreaming, or had confused Chris with some other man, before or after. Or was it Soonya who now told the truth? How corrosive was doubt! Meanwhile, Soonya was acting the scene, as though remembering, and now she wiped the tears from her eyes, one and the other, with her own handkerchief—real tears, as Laura could see.

"Such kindness," Soonya sobbed. "I am not having such kindness usually. So next night he come again. At first he is not there, and I am afraid he is not coming. Then he is coming and I run to meet him at table, feeling him so safely."

She paused, shook her head, and touched her handkerchief to her eyes. Outside the bird sang again, three notes three times, with the same piercing sweetness.

"And then?"

"Then we go sometimes to mountain for picnic, and sometimes we dance in evening. And we talk here. I do not know he is married. I dream so much. It is my fault, always dreaming. I dream he marries me and take me away to America. Ah, America is dream country! So first kissing, he show me, and afterwards we find small hooch house. When winter is coming with much snow we cannot go to mountain and not always at night to dance, if snow is deep and wind too cold. So, it is like this."

"I see," Laura said. "And did he never say he would marry you?"

"No, never. I have only hope."

"And when you knew you were pregnant?"

Soonya covered her face with her hands. Then she let

them drop into her lap. They lay there loosely, like lotus flowers, palms up.

"I was not wanting baby, I promise. Then he ask me please make baby for him."

"*What!*"

No, that could not be. Chris would never—

"But why?" she demanded.

Soonya knit her dark and mothlike brows. "He is saying that perhaps he die before he go home again. War is over but not end, he says. He will die in war, and leaving nothing of himself alive."

"And you gave him a child!"

"Because I love him very much."

She gazed deeply into Soonya's dark eyes and Soonya returned the deep look.

"I am thinking," Soonya said slowly, "I am always thinking he can never leave his child. So he will take me with child to America. I am same as wife if I have child. Then one day—a letter comes."

"What letter?" she asked under her breath.

"Your letter," Soonya said. "I know, because I read. When he is sleeping I read letter, taking from pocket. You are wishing him come home—to you. When I read, I know he will go. I put back letter. I say not one word. I only love better than before. And I hope. But hope is no good. He hears your calling. One day he is gone. Next day his friend is bringing me money and letter from him. In letter, he tells me his home where he is living with father and mother, if I am in trouble."

"It is where we live," Laura said. "His parents are dead now. Do you have the letter?"

"I have," Soonya said. "I keep it forever."

She opened the door of a small chest that stood in a shallow alcove, and inside that door she pulled out a drawer. Beneath other papers she searched, then turned, bewildered.

"It is not here! Then where is? I know! That naughty boy, he take! Sometimes I read it for him. Always so many questions, this boy. 'Who is my father, where is my father, why he is not writing, why he is not coming?' So I read letter to him. 'You don't touch,' I tell him."

"That is how he knew where to send his own letter."

She saw the whole story now. But what had she written to Chris so that he left these two here behind him? And had she made it up to him? No child—no child!

She was distracted by Soonya's sobbing again, a quiet soft sobbing.

"Please don't," she said. "I can't blame you. I do blame him. He should have known, should have taken thought."

Soonya lifted her head with sudden spirit.

"No blaming him. It is blame for you."

"I? But I didn't know."

"Such letter from you," Soonya said.

She did remember the letter. It had been her twenty-third birthday, a chill November day. She had gone upstairs to her room in her parents' house in New York to dress for the birthday party her mother had planned for her. Her windows faced Gramercy Park, and the sight of gray rain pelting the windowpane and dimming the empty park sent a chill of loneliness through her body. Three years ago to the day Chris and she had walked across that park together, she twenty that day, and they had walked hand in hand for the first time, both shy, both in a tumult of feeling, each reaching somehow for the other. But it had been too soon, she fearful of committing herself before she went back to the university and her dreamed-of career, and Chris saying nothing except to ask her huskily if she would write to him at college.

Neither of them thought of Korea. Indeed, neither knew anything about this small, troubled and distant country. She had given her promise, and had not kept it very well. She had written cool, short letters, still shrinking from commitment, for that was the time when she had come deeply under the influence of the famous oceanographer, Don Lawson, and he was persuading her to accompany him and three other scientists on an ocean expedition, her first, to collect algae from the sea floor. Young as she was—but had she ever been really young? That was the penalty a woman paid for having what men called "a man's brain," although nothing infuriated her more than the idea that brains belonged only to men, as though nature bestowed brains by sex instead of by chance and design of genes. Was it her fault that she, the girl, was the brilliant one in her family?

Yes, she remembered that twenty-third birthday. Sitting at her window with all those somber thoughts, she had been swept by such a rush of longing for Chris, whose last three letters she had not answered because they told her nothing, that she rose and went to her desk and wrote him a hasty letter, impassioned as she had never been before.

"Dear, dear Chris, I am twenty-three today, and have you forgotten? At any rate, there is no letter, though I've waited all day for a word from you—even that you might telephone, though that's difficult. Have you thought of me today? It is raining and cold and the wind is blowing the dead leaves in the park. When are you coming home? What will you be like, I wonder? Will you be changed? Am I changed? I don't think so, only older, and more sure of what I want. If I hear from you soon, I won't go on the deep-sea exploration I've been half planning with Don and the others . . . Write me a real letter, Chris! Or have you decided to reenlist? In which case I'll go with Don."

She could almost remember the words. No answer had come and she had let her heart grow still, had gone on the trip with Don, and while he had done his deep-sea diving for algae she had collected her plankton in a net attached to a nylon rope, the rope attached to the stern of the yacht that a millionaire friend of Don's had lent them. Hour after hour, day after day, she sat on the deck in her swimming suit, altogether a scientist, the men thought, and only she knew better. *Why did Chris not write?* She telephoned home every third day.

"No letter, Mother?"

"None from Korea, dear."

Then when she reached home, Chris was there. He had simply come home. Yes, he said, he had planned to ask for an extended service in Korea, if not a reenlistment, but her letter had brought him home. Now, eleven years later, she understood why the extension instead of reenlistment. The latter could have meant Europe instead of Asia, and it was Asia he wanted, Asia who sat here before her now in the graceful shape of a strange and beautiful woman.

"For you he leave me," Soonya said, and sighed.

She folded small pleats in the soft silk of her skirt, musing upon what thoughts Laura did not know. The long, straight lashes lay upon cheeks delicately pink, and an old fear crept into Laura's heart. Was it true, perhaps, that even Chris might prefer a woman who could and would devote her entire being, body and brain, to him? They had argued it more than once, she lying in his arms, wholly his, and yet never wholly his, as they both knew. For the hour of love would pass and then and always there would arise in her that cosmic curiosity of the superior brain, the eternal questioner, knowing neither sex nor self, but only the necessity for discovering truth in the universe. She could and did forget him for hours on end. Even for days she could forget him.

But Chris could laugh at her. "Remember me, sweetheart? Your husband! Give the old ocean a rest, will you? Let's fly to the Bahamas!"

Fly they often did, she always with a sense of guilt which she resented, for surely she had the same right to be an individual that he had. He forgot her without compunction when he was in one of his campaigns, and if they did end in the White House someday, as she had every confidence they would, Chris being what he was, he would be compelled to forget her, and she would understand as she understood now. She did not mind being forgotten—no, let her be truthful with herself—she was even glad to be forgotten, so that she too could forget and turn to her own work.

She was startled out of the deep reverie into which Soonya's comment had plunged her by a woman's voice from outside the house, a loud, scolding old voice, shouting Korean words as though she spat them at someone. In reply she heard another voice, a clear young voice, answering with laughter.

Soonya lifted her head and Laura met her eyes with her own full gaze. "I want to see the boy," she said.

Soonya rose to her feet and moved to the garden entrance, her feet silent beneath her long full skirt. She paused, her hand on the lintel and turned her head to look at Laura.

"I don't come back today," she said. "I send him to you alone."

She walked away then, and Laura saw her flowing rose red skirt moving among the trees and disappearing behind a clump of weeping willows that hung above a small oval pool.

How long she waited she did not know. As though I had been waiting all my life, she thought, but perhaps it was only a few minutes. The garden was silent, the bird flown, and she sat, tense and motionless. Would the boy come from the garden or from the shoji closed behind her? The house was silent, too, as though she alone were there. What if Soonya had betrayed her, had taken the boy away somewhere and left her here to wait and go away at last in despair?

Then she saw him. He came from the side of the house and stood before her, the garden his background. She felt her breath caught in her throat. The boy might have been Chris himself at twelve, a tall, clean-limbed boy, barefoot, barelegged, wearing blue shorts and a white sports shirt, both ragged, both not too clean. But the dark straight hair was neatly combed and still wet. Chris himself, she thought, except the eyes, the olive skin. Not his mouth, though. This was Soonya's soft mouth—

"Good morning, madame," the boy said.

He stood waiting, shy but not ill at ease, wearing a bright, interested look, an excitement, but controlled. A boy too wise for his years? Scarcely a child, at least!

"Good morning," she said. "I'm afraid I don't know your name."

"My father name—Christopher. I am Kim Christopher."

"Your English is good," she said.

He came in now and sat down on the cushion where Soonya had sat. A polite boy, she thought, very handsome, but wearing some sort of mask, a protection, perhaps. If it was difficult for her, it was also difficult for him.

"We have your letter," she went on. "He—your—your father, would like to have come but just now he is in a political campaign and could not get away. I am here in his stead."

She made up her mind not to treat him as a child, yet she was not sure he understood. If he did not, he concealed ignorance behind courtesy.

"My father—he is well?"

"Yes, very well."

"You have new picture?"

"Yes."

She opened her handbag and took out the picture she kept there of Chris, the one she had shown Soonya. Each birthday she renewed it, and since his birthday had been only a month ago, his face, resolute and cheerful, looked out at her exactly as he was. The boy took it eagerly in both hands.

"Hair is white!" he exclaimed.

"Only a little at the sides," she said.

"He is not old."

"No, but not quite young."

"He is beautiful," he murmured, and then lifted his beautiful eyes to question her. "May I keep picture?"

She put down reluctance. "Yes, if you like. Or shall I send you a larger one?"

"This one, please." He considered the face again. "He not want me?"

She countered. "Do you want to leave your mother?"

He was as clever. "I wish also my father."

"How can we manage that?" she asked. It startled her somehow that he spoke English so well.

"What my father says, I do. I belong father, not mother."

"Yet you are all she has."

"She is woman. She must do he say. If he tell me come, she must also."

"What if he wishes you to stay with her?"

He threw out his hands in a gesture of despair. "Here I am nothing—nothing. Supposing he send money for school, still I am nothing. I am not Korean. I am foreign. My father American. Why am I born?"

So might Chris have spoken, young and rebellious, impetuous and heartbroken. She put out her hand and touched his arm. "It is only that we don't know what to do. Tell me—you do love your mother? She is kind to you?"

He drew himself away from the hand resting on his arm. "I love, I hate."

"She is very gentle. Why do you hate her?"

He did not reply. He sat staring into the garden, not moody so much as trying to control himself. What was he suppressing, what angry words and resentful feelings, and against whom?

"Will you tell me what you are thinking?" she said at last.

"No," he said firmly. He got to his feet abruptly and made a short bob of a bow. "If you have nothing more for say to me, please excuse me, madame."

He ran from the room and into the garden so swiftly that it was as though he had never come. She waited for a moment longer and then rose to her feet. The shoji opened at the same instant, as if she had been watched, and the old woman was there. She went out, the old woman following her to the gate, and got into the taxicab she had not dismissed.

"Back to the hotel," she said.

The spring day had turned suddenly to summer. When she reached her room she was weary and hot. The air was oppressive, and from her window she saw black thunder-clouds hanging over the crest of the mountain. She felt far away, infinitely far from Chris, and she went impulsively to the telephone. After half an hour's effort she reached the overseas operator, but she could get no further.

"Sorry," the Korean girl's voice sang, "we have transmission difficulty."

Transmission difficulty! She yielded to necessity, gave up the thought of hearing Chris' voice, and pondered the possibility of a letter. No, it was too soon to write. She did not know enough yet of the boy to write about him. And what if she never saw him again?

A roar of thunder rumbled over the sky. Sleep, that was her only escape, a hot bath and then sleep. An hour later, washed and cooled, her hair brushed and braided, she lay on her bed asleep, while the storm broke over the city.

When she woke it was twilight. Thunder and rain had passed and she felt refreshed and very hungry. She had eaten nothing since morning, she now remembered, and she rose and dressed and went downstairs to the dining room. It was late, the dinner hour was nearly over, but two young men in American uniforms were seated by the window. They looked up as she came in, observed her with interest, as she perceived, and followed her with their eyes while she sat down at the table next to theirs. They were finishing their dinner, but they lingered over coffee, discussing her, as she more than suspected. She smiled as one of them caught her glance, and immediately the two of them rose as one and came to her table.

"Excuse me," the younger one said, the red-haired one, "but haven't we met you somewhere?"

She laughed. "I think not, since I came only yesterday."

"Then may we meet you now?"

"Why not? I'm Mrs. Chris Winters."

He groaned. "I knew it. We have no luck! I'm Jim

Traynor, and this is Lieutenant Lucius Brown. We're stationed here, and though we're not supposed to be in the hotels . . . well, here we are. Why? Because the beef is good—shipped in from Japan. Kobe beef, beer-fed and hand-massaged, so it melts in your mouth. I see you're eating fish—a mistake, ma'am!"

"May we sit down?" Lieutenant Brown inquired.

He was correct and spare in looks and speech, with the mark of his Boston breeding on him. Jim, in contrast, had clearly grown up on some teeming city street—Chicago, perhaps—and was immediately and inevitably "Jim" in his leisure moments, without regard to military rank.

"Please," she said. "I was just wondering what I could do with an evening."

They sat down. "Ever been at Walker Hill?" Jim asked.

"I haven't been anywhere," she said.

The two men looked at each other. "Then we'll take her to Walker Hill," Jim exclaimed.

"Walker Hill," Brown agreed.

An hour later she found herself again seated between two young men, but in what a different scene! She saw a large room, filled with small tables at which American men sat alone, in two's or four's, or with Korean girls, loud and raucous music contending with the clatter of dishes and shouts from the bar. At one end a dancer performed in the scantiest of clothing, a Korean girl, she saw, but imitating with a grotesque grace the antics of a watusi. On the floor American servicemen danced with Korean girls who wore short tight Western dresses, their hair curled and piled on their heads in monstrous exaggeration.

"Where are we?" she asked in bewilderment.

Jim laughed. "Don't mind the girls, ma'am. They think they're being American. They see the old movie magazines and try to look like the Hollywood stars. Try to act like them, too, but—" He shook his head.

Lieutenant Brown continued for him. "It's an interesting phenomenon, Mrs. Winters. The girls, who have never seen real American girls, think that all American women are like the movie queens. So they make themselves up as nearly as possible to look like the American stars. Then, reasoning that such stars must behave as they look, they—these Korean girls—conduct themselves with a freedom that our girls, even in Hollywood, would never imagine."

"I had a girl yell at me the other day across the street," Jim began and, catching his friend's eye, he stopped abruptly.

At this moment a girl, exquisite as a madonna, approached them and sidled up to Jim.

"Me hot body," she whispered.

"Get out," he muttered between his teeth.

Laura laughed aloud. "Really, you are too attractive!" Her laughter broke their reserve. Here was a woman, a lady, an American to whom they could talk.

"Gee, Mrs. Winters," Jim said, "you've no idea. If a fellow takes a walk these girls are at him like flies. Why, I've even had one reach out right on the street and grab my zipper—"

"Spare us, boy," the other broke in quickly. "But it's true, Mrs. Winters. One can't blame the men entirely, I assure you. It's no temptation to me. I'm engaged to a wonderful girl in Boston, but Jim, here . . ." he grinned.

Jim growled.

"Cut it out, now."

Lieutenant Brown went on. "Take the young fellows from little towns and farms, though, kids of eighteen, say, to twenty-five or so. They simply give up. It's not that the girls are so tempting but the fellows are in a rebellious mood anyway and ready for anything. They don't like it here, they don't know why they're here, they're homesick. Look at that kid."

That kid was a scrawny lad not out of his teens, who shuffled past them, embracing a pretty Korean girl, her body pressed to his, her face in his neck.

"That kid," Lieutenant Brown was saying. "At home no girl would look at him—none that he wants, he's homely—as—as—"

"Hell," Jim put in.

Lieutenant Brown went on. "But he always hankers after the prettiest and most popular girl, the one he can't get. Take that little cat that he's hugging now—"

Jim interrupted. "She's told him he's the handsomest male that ever crossed her path, and he believes it. He's been wanting some girl to say that to him ever since he was in kindergarten and the little girl next door spat at him."

She listened thoughtfully. "It wouldn't matter except that perhaps there'll be a child."

"Plenty of those," Jim said. "You should see them when you go out in the villages."

The racking music was banging at her ears. A girl was singing a torch song in a kind of English.

"Does she know what she's singing?" she asked.

Jim shook his head. "Not a word. She's learned it like a parrot, from some broken-down record she's picked up."

She was silent in the midst of the din of song and tinny piano and shuffling feet. Would she or would she not disclose to these two why she was here? Could they be of help to her? Yet, how could they be? Before she could answer her own questions she was startled to see Mr. Choe, tall and elegant, enter the door. He stood there, his eyes searching the crowd until they lit upon her. Then he came to her swiftly, avoiding with grace collisions with dancing couples oblivious to all save their own movements.

"Ah, you are here," he exclaimed when he had reached Laura's side. "I have been looking for you."

"How did you find me?" she asked.

"At the hotel they knew." He stood, waiting, and she introduced him perforce to the two Americans.

Lieutenant Brown shook hands. Jim nodded.

"Will you sit down?" Laura said.

He remained standing. "I have been commanded to give you an invitation and to ask that you accept it."

"Really? Where?"

"Kim Soonya invites you to see her performance at The House of Flowers. You will be the first American ever to see it."

She rose at once. "You will excuse me, gentlemen? I have a special reason for accepting this invitation."

"Certainly," said Lieutenant Brown, and "Sure," Jim said, as both rose to their feet.

She looked back when she reached the door and saw their surprised eyes, still fixed upon her.

"I was afraid I could not find you before curfew," Mr.

Choe said. They were in his comfortable limousine, the chauffeur pressing his way through the crowds. "Happily, at the hotel they could tell me where you were, since they keep knowledge of all foreign guests and where each is at all times."

"Why?"

"These are unsettled days. In case of sudden trouble, such as the unexpected overthrow of government, for example, we must know where each person is who is not native to our country. This is for your own protection."

"Are you expecting an overthrow of government?" she asked.

"We must expect anything," he replied. "I myself think we are safe for one more year at least. But one never knows what may be boiling beneath our nation's surface. The times are evil, Mrs. Winters. Our traditional government was a monarchy. This government the Japanese destroyed when they took over our country and compelled our Crown Prince to marry a Japanese princess. For many decades we were subject to cruel military rule by the Japanese. Now, under American advice, we are trying to establish a government we do not understand fully, a democracy which is not native to us. Inevitably there is contention between ambitious men, each with his own followers in the army. Peace is far off. Our young people are rebellious, especially since the trade treaties with Japan. They are tempted by Communist propaganda from the North urging unification of the country at all costs."

It was a long speech to which she listened with attention, understanding fully the portent of his words and yet so concentrated on her own mission that her thoughts could focus only on one small boy who was her husband's son.

"In that case what will happen to children like Kim Christopher?"

Mr. Choe answered without hesitation. "They will be killed. Many have already died."

"What do you mean?" she demanded.

"There was a period in the last decade, Mrs. Winters, when mysteriously many of these children fathered by your men disappeared."

"Disappeared?"

"Yes. They died. In many ways. Also, some of the male children were castrated. Not only here but also in Japan. It is true. This was done. You will blame us very much and we are to blame, but you must remember that we are an ancient people, and very proud. In fact, you have only to see what takes place in your own country when two different races meet by blood. Many murders—"

She saw his pale stern profile, handsome and remote as an Asian god, staring into the lighted street. In this moment she made a decision, involuntary with horror. "Then, Mr. Choe, you must help me to get Kim Christopher out of this country."

"It is his only safety," he replied.

The car drew up before a brightly lit gateway, set in a brick wall, decorated with painted flowers. Two girls in Korean dress waited with bouquets in their hands.

"Ah, we are expected," Mr. Choe said.

They descended from the car, the girls pressed forward, presenting the bouquets.

"Welcome, welcome," they said, one after the other.

"Thank you," she replied, and her arms laden with flowers, she followed them into the courtyard and up marble steps into an entrance hall. The hall led throughout the house, or so it appeared, with shoji opening left and right. At the end of the hall and coming toward her she saw Soonya, dressed in a brocaded satin skirt and a bodice of pale gold. Her dark hair was piled on her head instead of hanging in the long thick braid, and as she came near, Laura's heart chilled. This was surely the most beautiful woman she had ever seen, more beautiful now, she hoped, than when Chris had known her. But the pale fine smooth skin, the classic Asian features, the great dark eyes, these would never change.

Meanwhile, Soonya came forward and took away the flowers and gave them to a small dainty girl in a green silk skirt and bodice.

"Too many flowers," she said to Laura. "They choke you. Come, please."

She took Laura's hand, and holding it delicately, she led the way into a large room. Here men were seated on satin floor cushions, and beside each man was a girl, who served him with food, lit his cigarettes and fanned him from time to time, laughed dutifully at his jokes and endured his caresses. At one side of the room was a floor cushion of red velvet with a seat back, and here Soonya now invited Laura to sit. It was her own usual seat, it seemed, and when Laura protested, Soonya forced her gently down with her two hands on Laura's shoulders so that perforce she must obey. Nearby she seated Mr. Choe and a girl came to serve him as the other men were served.

Soonya, however, all now being in order, did not seat herself. Instead she walked with dignity to a small platform, stepped upon it, and waited. It was not obvious for whom she waited, but whomever it was, she grew impatient and clapped her hands. Immediately a boy walked in from the wings, a Korean boy in the white robes of a man, a wig of straight black hair on his head and a high horsehair hat. He carried a sort of lute such as Laura had never seen before and he seated himself cross-legged on the floor and played upon the strings. After a brief prelude, Soonya began to sing. She had a soaring rich soprano voice, very pure and clear, and the winding Korean melody gave it full display.

Laura listened, enchanted and wistful. How could she compete with this woman? Why had Chris hidden Soonya in his memory all these years? If he had nothing to hide would he not surely have told her? In the midst of these sorrowful questions, she noticed that the boy had lifted his head and was looking at her, his fingers busy with the strings. Then she saw the eyes. They were the eyes of Kim Christopher.

She leaned forward to Mr. Choe. "Why have you brought me here?"

"She asked me to do so," he replied.

"And why, and why?"

He waved his hand toward Soonya. "She is singing. Let us listen," he replied, and she was silenced.

"Did you never see this boy before?"

She put the question to Mr. Choe as they drove back to the hotel in his limousine. She had waited only until

Soonya had finished her songs. Then, before they could meet, she had asked to leave.

Mr. Choe had protested. "There is usually a small feast on such evenings."

"I can return quite well alone," she had replied.

"No, no."

He had left then, the girl carrying his topcoat and hat to the car and handing them to him, and he had rewarded her with money, for which she had bowed deeply again and again.

"I never saw this boy before," he now replied.

"He is my husband's son."

He turned a startled face. "Not this boy! He is Korean!"

"She made him look so tonight, for some reason of her own. What is that reason?"

"A devious woman," he said. "But a beautiful woman is perhaps always devious."

"How will she use this boy?" she asked.

"Who knows? Perhaps she will make him her business manager. Perhaps he will find clients for her."

She was blunt. "Is this place of hers anything more than a brothel?"

He replied somewhat reluctantly. "Perhaps now—perhaps one would call it that. You must understand, however, that we older peoples are more worldly wise than you are. Or perhaps it is only that we like an ordered society, and to attain permanent order we have based our laws and customs upon human nature. In your country your laws are corrective, whereas ours seek to follow human nature. For example, we know that men need women as women do not need men. Men are quite simple, in fact. We need women as our wives and the mothers of our children. We also need women as sexual instruments. It is seldom that these two functions can be fulfilled by the same women. We accept this and we allow women to divide themselves. Those who wish to have the stable lives of wife and mother give themselves only in marriage. Those who for various reasons in accordance with their own natures do not need this stability move easily into prostitution. By the way, our word is not so harsh. We speak of these women as flowers rather than prostitutes."

Her reply to his philosophizing was direct. "A prostitute is a prostitute."

He replied gently. "Does it matter what they are called?"

She caught his sidewise glance. "To us it does. We call a spade a spade."

"Ah, yes, I remember—regardless of feelings!"

"The truth cannot be hidden."

"No more than the nature of man," he agreed, "but I think we are more truthful than you are. We accept the prostitute as a part of society. She has her recognized place. At the same time we consider her feelings. We call her a flower."

They fell into silence, but when they had reached the hotel he held her in the lobby, now empty except for the clerk at the desk.

"What do you propose to do with the boy?" he asked.

"When I came here," she said, "my only intention was

to put him in a school and give him an education . . . fit him to earn his living in some honorable way."

"Make a Korean out of him," he amended.

"He is a Korean, isn't he? He was born here."

"You may call him a Korean but we do not. For us he is the son of his father. He is American. Why does his father not claim him? Then all problems would be solved."

How could she explain to him? "You have been in my country . . ." she began.

"In your country all nationalities are mixed," he protested. "There can be no disgrace in being partly Korean. For us it is not the same. We are the oldest people in the world, the most civilized. When your ancestors were living in caves my ancestors were artists and scholars."

"Oh, I know," she retreated quickly. "I've been reading. It's not that. It's—"

He waited, tall, dignified, ready to be wounded and she felt pinned against the wall by his piercing steady gaze. She could not evade it. She was compelled to trust him.

"My husband is running for the governorship of our state. His opponents would delight in the story of this boy. I simply cannot see a fine career hopelessly lost because of a young man's silly mistake, made in a time when he was lonely and afraid he would never get home again."

"What you are saying is that you do not wish to take this boy home to his father, where he belongs."

"To us it is possible that he belongs here."

"Is he, a human being, to be caught between these possibles and impossibles? Ah, Mrs. Winters, you had better face the truth!"

They were interrupted by the entrance into the lobby of Lieutenants Brown and Traynor. Both were drunk.

"Here sh—she is," Jim shouted. "Been lookin' for you everywhere."

"Everywhere," Lieutenant Brown boomed in his deep bass.

"Let me see you to your room," Mr. Choe said hurriedly.

He stepped between her and the Americans, and holding her elbow he led her into the elevator and thence to the door of her room.

"Thank you," she said, with a small smile, feeling torn between irritation and amusement. "Thank you for delivering me from my own people."

He bowed and waited. She lifted her eyebrows.

"I wish to hear the door locked," he said.

"Oh—thank you again. And goodnight."

She closed the door and turned the lock. And then, without warning, an awareness of utter isolation fell upon her such as she felt only when, now and again, she was swimming at the bottom of the ocean, alone, surrounded by strange inhuman creatures. In that dim nether world, moving among species of life that were not hers, panic could seize her, which nevertheless she had learned to control. It had been necessary for her to accept the isolation if she were to pursue her way as an oceanographer. She had compromised only to the extent of never going alone to those depths. Now remembering, she recalled a certain afternoon. With her co-worker, John Wilton, by her side, she was swimming at seventy feet below the surface of the sea near the isle called Saboga to gather algae. The waving fronds of algae, a miniature forest moving to the rhythm of the surge currents, were a fairyland of trees, delicate as shadows, and yet in which she might easily be attacked by some sea creature, barracuda or shark. Watchful, she had continued her task, which had been to collect the many forms of algae for which they were searching, the healing qualities of which, so near to vegetable, so close to animal, might yet guarantee an eternal source of antibiotics for the healing of mankind. And then the strange enzymes, like hormones, able to change life itself, even sex—

She had dropped into a chair, musing, and now recalled herself.

What was she doing here, involved in a world she did not know and could not understand, alone, without Chris, among strangers who could not help her? She had no equipment to live in this world, much less to solve a problem which was not hers in the first place, and to which there seemed to be no solution. She struggled with the temptation simply to leave, go home, declare herself vanquished. After all, it was only one of the problems resulting from the upheavals of war and the compulsions of alien peoples thrown together by necessity.

At this moment, as though she had stretched out her hand for help, the telephone rang. She seized the receiver and heard clipped Korean English.

"Mrs. Christopha Wintah, please?"

"Yes?"

"Ovahsheas operatah, please."

And then before she could cry out, Chris's voice came across the oceans and out of the night. Miraculously it came, as though he were in the next room, rising and falling only slightly upon the waves of atmosphere.

"Laura?"

"Oh, Chris, how heavenly to hear you! I was beginning to feel so sorry for myself."

"When are you coming home?"

"Why, I don't know. I've only just got here. I've found the boy."

"What's he like?"

"Like you!"

Silence fell. She cried out against it.

"Chris?"

"Yes, I'm here . . ."

"I don't know what to do about him."

"Get him into a school somewhere and come home. I need you. Looks like I'll get the nomination."

"Oh, that's good news."

"A long way to go, though. Have you enough money?"

"Yes, plenty. I haven't begun to spend yet . . . I've seen Soonya, too."

"Does she want money?"

"She hasn't said so."

"If you are in trouble of any kind, remember to go to the American Embassy. That's what they're there for."

"It's not trouble I'm having . . . just that I don't quite know what to do next."

"Come home."

"No, now I'm here, I must do something about the boy."

"Shall I come?"

"No. Whatever needs to be done, I'll do."

There seemed nothing more to be said, but she clung to the receiver, longing to have him keep on talking.

"Chris, you didn't tell me how beautiful it is here . . . but strange. As to the people, I can't seem to lay hold of anything I understand. They think so differently from us."

"Get Americans to help you."

"All right, Chris."

His voice suddenly faded. He was speaking but she could not hear.

"Chris—Chris—" she cried, but there was no answer.

She could only hang up the receiver and go to bed.

In the morning it seemed a dream that she and Chris had actually talked across the oceans. Yet the conversation was clear in her memory. Get Americans, he had said, and with this direction she rose resolutely and set about the day.

"Where is the American Embassy?" she inquired at the desk an hour later.

"Across the street, please, madame," the clerk told her.

Across the street she went then and was ushered out of one office and into another, to talk at last with a cool middle-aged woman who spoke with a flat Ohio accent.

"Mrs. Winters? Sit down. How can I help you?"

She sat down. "I have come here to find a child—a half-American, Miss—"

"Pitman. Your husband's child?"

"How did you know?"

"You're not the first one. Not too many of you, either, and sometimes it's the man that comes looking for his own child. Not many of them, either. Mostly the children just grow up here."

"Does our government do nothing about them?"

"No, ma'am. We have no policy concerning their care. Our men are now in seven countries in Asia and we—"

"What is to become of the children?"

"I can't tell you. We have no policy—"

"You said that."

Miss Pitman began sorting papers. "If I can help you—"

"What is the best thing for me to do?"

"Depends on what you want to do."

"I don't know what I can do."

"Only one of two things, Mrs. Winters. You can leave him here or take him to the United States."

"What will happen to him if I leave him here? Put him in a boarding school, of course—"

"There are no boarding schools here, unless—how old is he?"

"Twelve."

"Then there are no boarding schools here. He doesn't qualify as an orphan, of course.

"What shall I do, then?"

"Forget him. That's what most other Americans do. Thousands of these children."

"What's to become of them?"

"Depends on what happens here. If there's a Communist invasion—might be, if we get so involved in Vietnam that we pull out too many men from here—they'll all be killed anyway, likely, or become Communists, since no one else seems to want them."

She watched Miss Pitman's spectacled face as she absorbed herself in some task having to do with the papers she was sorting.

"Miss Pitman, don't you care at all?"

"I can't afford to. There's nothing I can do."

"Is there nothing I can do at least about this one boy?"

Miss Pitman looked at her over the spectacles. "If your husband acknowledges paternity you can take him to the United States as an American citizen."

"Just like that?"

"Just like that."

She rose. "Thank you."

"Not at all."

That, then, was all she could do. She could forget him and go home, or she could let Chris declare himself the father and take him home with her. She would go back to the hotel and write Chris a letter, explaining how easy it would be for him merely to tell the truth, and then she could bring the boy to America. And take him home? Looking so much like Chris?

From the window in the room above hers in the hotel, Mr. Choe had watched her cross the street to the Embassy, had waited and had watched her return again. She must therefore be in her room now. It had been a long time since he had met and talked with an American woman, and vague memories stirred in him. Once when he had been at the University—it was in his senior year, he remembered —he had been deeply in love with a girl who now returned to his mind because she looked like this Mrs. Christopher Winters. True, her hair had not been red, nor was she perhaps so beautiful, but at the time he had thought her the most beautiful girl he had ever met. He had written home to his parents asking for permission to arrange a marriage with this American girl. To this they had replied with such agonized pleadings, such threats and tears ostentatiously staining the letter paper, that he had given up the hope, had finished his year and come home to marry the wife they had chosen for him long ago. His Korean wife had borne him an assorted number of daughters, and at last one son. She had married off the daughters in due course, had pampered the son into young adulthood and then had died, leaving Mr. Choe at his present loose ends. Now alone and ready to be distracted, he found himself torn in two directions, first by the beautiful courtesan, Soonya, and also by Mrs. Winters. He was a sensible man and he did not contemplate marriage to either of them. It is not necessary to marry a courtesan, although, to be sure, none of his overtures to Soonya had yet gained him more than a smile; and of course he could not marry an American already married, even if he had been so inclined. Nevertheless he was intensely aware of them both as women, and his imagination was teased by their astounding connection with the same American man, a man who must have a peculiar personal power and who now apparently was struggling for political power. He was fascinated also by the contrast between these two women, the one so feminine, so finished a courtesan, and the other one of those slim man-women to be found, he believed, only in America, women who, with burnished hair and glowing eyes and superb figures, have the brains of a man. It was this kind of contrast which he had been trying to describe to Mrs. Winters only the night before. She had listened so attentively that he wondered if he might hope to continue the conversation into an area of intimacy after he had escorted her to the door. She had remained unconscious of his intent, however, and he would have to wait until his spy in the American Embassy could report to him the reason for her visit there. Meanwhile, he decided, he would visit Kim Soonya and if possible see for himself this half-American son of whom she alternately complained and boasted.

An hour later he was seated in Soonya's private sitting room in The House of Flowers, and at his request she was telling him all about Christopher Winters. She spoke Korean with an elegance which he admired and which he attributed to the fact that she allowed herself association only with *yangban* Korean men of high quality, like himself.

"It is not possible to describe how it happened," she said.

She was seated on a floor cushion and she leaned her elbows on the low table between them. She wore a green skirt and a pale yellow bodice, the sleeves of which, falling away, showed arms of milk-white skin and delicate bone shape. Her hands were exquisite, small and soft, the fingers tapered and the nails like polished mother-of-pearl.

"In the first place, I am not, as you know, of the low family of most girls who accept Americans. My parents were educated, my father a teacher, and I was their only child. I have told you of the day our house was bombed and my father killed, and how my mother and I, helpless and frightened, wandered the streets, searching for shelter and food. And you know, too, how the foreign soldiers came into the city like locusts over a field. Not one of us escaped—not even my mother." She hid her eyes with her hand for a moment and then went on. "I cannot speak of that. But I saw I had to save my mother. I joined the other girls orphaned by war and made a little money singing and dancing. I rented a room where my mother lived while I worked. I was more delicate than the other girls and I became often ill, and could not work at all. They were kind and they fed me from their own food. But I could not expect them to care for my mother. One night, dreading it very much, I went into a place where the Americans gathered to dance—we were afraid of Americans most of all—and I saw a young man sitting alone at a table. He had a beautiful sad face, he was very young, and he was not dancing. I hated their dancing. They did in their dancing, those Americans, what other men do only in bed. I thought if I sat down beside this lonely man, the other men would stay away from me. And my friend Dolly persuaded me also. Thus it began."

"With such beginning," Mr. Choe said, since she had

paused for a long time and it seemed as though she would not go on again, "how did it end in a child?"

She leaned against the back of her seat now, and twisted her hands together in her silken lap. "I was very afraid to let him go," she confessed. "He did indeed protect me from the others. From those coarse, loud young men, he protected me. They did not approach me when they knew of him, and so at last we came to live together in a small house. He paid the key money to the landlord, one hundred and fifty American dollars, and this money the landlord used for lending, retaining the interest, and giving back again the initial sum to the American when he went home. To maintain us the American bought with his own money goods at the PX—you know PX?"

Mr. Choe nodded.

"And I sold such goods on the black market and bought our food, and such things as we needed. It is the usual way to live with American men. Also he had some money beside, sent to him in letters from his parents, but he did not like to give it to me. He said it was forbidden to use here because men from the North came as spies into our South and bought this American money to spend in other countries for their own reasons. American money is good anywhere in the world."

"The child is nevertheless not explained," Mr. Choe observed.

Soonya blushed deeply. She was so fair that the slightest blush showed, rose-pink, on her face, and now it was more than that.

"I learned to love the American," she said shyly. "He

became necessary to me. I had never loved any man before, but he was kind to me, a good man, and he did not live with other women, only me. I asked him to marry me, and he said 'perhaps,' but never did he say he truly would. Then I thought to myself that if I gave him a child, surely he would take the child and me also to his own country. When I told him the child would be born, he was angry with me and yet he was eager, so that I could not be sure whether I had done well to have a child. When it was born and we saw it was a boy, I still could not be sure. Sometimes the father was pleased and made happy, sometimes he was sad. Then one day he went away. All this time I had not lived with my own mother and I did not allow her to come to the American. I told him I had no parents."

"Why?"

"Because I wanted him to think I depended only on him. I thought he would not leave me alone. You know that he did leave. But I did not tell you he wrote to me from America, one letter. He told me where he lived, and said he missed me so much he might just come back one day, quite suddenly. I kept it in my room at my mother's house."

"But he made no promises."

"He never did."

"Did you know he was married already?"

"No, he never told me."

"You did not ask?"

"I thought he would tell me. Perhaps I was afraid and didn't want to know."

"And you still—ah—love him?"

"No," she said. "Long ago I ceased to love him."

"And so?"

"He must pay well for the child," she said.

Outside the shoji, hidden behind a gardenia bush, Kim Christopher listened. He had never heard the story of how he was born, and had only recently found out his father's name. Before that he had known only that his father was an American and this made him a stranger, one of the new people here in Korea.

"These new people, what shall we do with them?"

It was what people said on the streets and in the shops. Sometimes the talk went further, sometimes it became dangerous and frightened him. A proud old man had shouted aloud one day in the midst of a crowd, "They must be thrown into the sea if there is no other way of ridding ourselves of these new people!" And he could not go to school, and anyway, the Korean schoolchildren laughed at him and pointed their fingers at him. "Your mother is a whore because your father is American," they shouted. "Only whores sleep with Americans," they shouted, and they called him "Round Eyes" or "Big Nose," though his eyes were not round nor his nose big. From the very first moment of his memory he knew that he had no place in this country, though he had a grandmother who was kind to him one day and cruel the next, and a mother whom he loved because she was beautiful but hated because she lived her life apart from them. It was only yesterday that he had for the first time been inside this other house of hers, filled with beautiful girls. She had brought him here, she had seen him bathed, his hair washed and cut short, she had told him that from now on he would help her in The House of Flowers. He should learn the business, she said, but what did she mean by that? That was what he had not yet discovered. He liked to sing and he liked to play the lute. He had learned these by himself, out of love for her, because she could sing so sweetly. He earned a little money sometimes by sweeping the streets in front of outdoor shops and he had bought the lute, a cheap one and not very good but it was a lute. And he had been proud last night when she told him to sing for the guests.

There had been many men last night after the entertainment was over who had come to see the girls and gone with them into small rooms and shut the doors. But no man went into his mother's room. He did not sleep there, either. He slept in the gateman's room, an old man who snored all night. Then this morning the tall man named Mr. Choe had come to see his mother and he had hidden himself in the garden just to listen and to watch. Now Mr. Choe was going away, and he waited as still as a rabbit until he was gone. When his mother was alone, an old woman came to offer her tea and his mother shouted in a voice he had never heard before.

"Get gone. Leave me alone!"

Now the old woman too was gone and he heard sobbing. He peered out of the gardenia bush and saw his mother sitting there alone on the floor cushion. She had folded her arms on the low table and had laid her head down, and she was sobbing softly to herself. Hesitantly, he moved toward her.

"Now I know," he said, in Korean.

Soonya lifted her head, "Know what?"

"Who I am," he said.

"You are my son," she said. "Have you not always known that?"

"I know my American father's name," he went on.

"What does it matter what his name is, since he does not recognize you? He has never sent money for you, he has never asked whether you live."

He glanced at her from under his lashes. Did she know or did she not know about the letter?

"I know where he lives in America," he said.

She suddenly screamed at him. "And you wrote him a letter! You searched in my private desk and stole his letter to me and wrote to him against me!"

"I did not—I did not write against you!"

He was stammering as he always did when she frightened him. He was frightened now, and seeing the fear in his eyes she flew at him and slapped him on both cheeks, this side and that, this side and that. He cowered down to the floor. He was not afraid of her, he always told himself when he was not with her; and why should he be afraid of her now when he was nearly as tall as she? It was simply that if she, his mother, did not love him, then who could love him? He was utterly alone in a land strange because he was a stranger. Crouched on the floor, his arms over his head to shield himself, he felt her foot kick his buttocks.

"Get out of my sight," she said. "After all I have done for you, you hate me!"

He got up, sobbing. "I don't hate you."

"You do," she insisted. "You love your father who has never cared whether you live or die."

They faced each other and suddenly he felt the strength of a new anger fiery in his veins. "Must I grow up a nobody? What shall I do with myself when I am a man? Am I to be a ragpicker? A beggar?"

"You will help me in this house," she told him. "You will do whatever I say."

"A servant!"

"A servant," she shouted. "Yes, a servant, if that is all you are fit to be!"

They stood staring at each other, and suddenly he realized as never before that he was her son, too. The face before him was like his face. He saw the resemblance, though dreaming so long of his American father he had imagined himself American.

"What do you want me to be?" he demanded.

Anger faded. She sighed and sank down on the floor cushion again. "You can go into business with me. You have a fine voice and you play the lute well enough."

"Girl business," he muttered.

"Only beginning thus," she said. Who could have imagined that this same voice had screamed at him a few minutes ago? "You can learn how to keep accounts and at least manage the business. When I retire it will be yours."

He considered. He was no child, he had never been a child, and he knew that boys younger than he, whose fathers had been like his, hung about the American camps and offered their sisters to the men for a commission. One such boy was his best friend, if he could be said to have a friend. Only yesterday, when they had been playing jackstones outside the gate of the barricade surrounding the camp, the game was stopped because a trio of young

American men came out and the boy had leaped to his feet to shout at them.

"Hi, hi, wanta girl? Nice girl, sexy, sexy."

The men had shoved him out of the way and they had resumed their game. But sometimes the young Americans stopped. Sometimes, even, they seemed to stop just to make friends with the boys. One he well remembered had offered him money to get him into The House of Flowers. But Kim Christopher had never been there himself and was much too afraid of his mother to try. So he had refused.

"What are you thinking?" his mother asked him.

He shrugged his shoulders and without answering he slouched away. She shouted after him in renewed anger. "Come back . . . answer me! I'll beat you!"

He did not obey. Suddenly he was not afraid of her. Suddenly he knew he would never be afraid of her again. He knew now what she wanted him to be—a boy to serve her, a man to sell women for her. Somehow he must find his father.

Laura was lying on her bed when she heard a knock at the door, a tentative, hesitating knock. She opened her eyes and did not rise. She was very weary, a fatigue that had nothing to do with her body except that the weariness of her spirit, pervading, made her listless. The knock came again, this time more clearly. She rose and put on her dressing gown. There stood the boy. Had she guessed a hundred times she could not have imagined it would be he. He stood mutely looking at her, this morning in his usual shirt and shorts, bare-legged, his feet in straw sandals.

"Come in, Kim Christopher," she said, uncertain and surprised.

He came in and stood looking about him.

"Please sit down," she said.

She sat down in one chair and he took the other. The light from the window fell on his face and on his cheeks she saw the slightly red lines of a blow. "What is the matter with your face?" she asked.

"My mother—"

He lifted his right hand and imitated the blow.

"Oh, no," she breathed. She rose from her seat impulsively and went to him, and putting out her hand she smoothed his cheek. The skin was fine and soft. That was the Korean side of him, she thought. "Why was she angry?"

He was not sure how far his English would go. He made an effort now. "My mother—she—she—talk I stay by her."

"You mean in The House of Flowers?"

He nodded. "Work."

"Do you want to work there?"

"No."

She gazed into his face, striving to divine his thoughts.

"You love your mother?"

Obviously he understood more than he could speak. "Sometimes," he said.

"Sometimes," she repeated. "Is she kind to you?"

He hesitated. "No school."

"Your grandmother. Is she kind?"

He leaped to his feet and imitated beating. "She do so on me."

He sat down again and folded his hands on his young bony knees. He stared at the floor, his face impassive, the long straight black lashes lying on his cheeks. How like he was to Chris and how unlike! What was to become of him?

"Suppose I send you to school here, Kim Christopher," she said.

He shook his head in his decisive fashion.

"No?"

He lifted the long lashes. "America," he said simply.

She sighed, pondering the puzzle of this child born too soon for the world.

"My father, please," he said.

"I know," she said. "I know, I know."

She got up restlessly, and going to the window she stood gazing out over the alien city. Yes, but it was not a matter to be settled by one child. There was Chris to be thought of, not to mention herself. Well, she could put herself aside, for in her detached life as a scientist people were beyond the horizon, and in her other life, her life with Chris, what people thought meant nothing. But Chris, whose life and career depended upon the whims, the prejudices, the narrow likes and dislikes of a constituency . . . what would they say if she brought home a lad who looked enough like Chris to start gossip flaming across a state—nay, a nation! Such flames could destroy him and make ashes of his life. Ah, it was only the child who was wholly innocent.

She turned impulsively and went to him and took his hand. How shabby he was in those sorry clothes he wore! She must take him now and get him some decent things to wear. Then she'd take him to lunch downstairs and give him a full meal. He was bone thin, his ribs defined in ridges under his skin, that wonderful skin, smooth and cream-pale—Asia's gift.

"Kim Christopher, we'll buy you some new clothes. Show me a shop."

She fingered his shirt, shaking her head, conveying disapproval. "Ah," he exclaimed, enlightened, and seizing her hand, he led her downstairs and then pointed up the street.

"Clothes?" she inquired.

"Yes, yes," he said eagerly and within the hour he was outfitted, three changes of everything and a crimson jersey for cool days.

"Put these on," she said, and when he had done so, she took the garments he had been wearing between thumb and finger and threw them to one side.

"No more those," she told him. "They are rags."

He was shocked, she could see, but she was adamant, and led him away in triumph, proud of his looks. If Chris could see him now! She checked herself. She must not be carried away by her own enthusiasm. True, he was beautiful. But that was to be expected, wasn't it, with Chris for his father—and yes, let her be generous, with Soonya for his mother. Yet surely there was a special alchemy here, for she had not seen Korean children as beautiful as this one, nor indeed the children in her own city, with whom she had grown out of childhood. It was not merely a matter of feature and coloring. There was an added grace, a combination perhaps of grace with strength. Kim Christopher was more graceful than the American child, and stronger than the Korean. She thought of her sea plants, those bridging creatures, the delicacy of the waving fronds of seaweed somehow verging into the strong life of the animal.

She recalled her thoughts. Kim Christopher was waiting before her in quiet patience, standing for her judgment.

"Good," she said. "Now you look handsome."

"American?" he inquired hopefully.

"Yes," she said, in truth and untruth. Very American here in Korea, but when she got him home—if she took him home—she knew he would look Asian. Where, where was his country?

"Let us go back to the hotel and have luncheon," she said.

She saw the instant she entered the dining room that Mr. Choe was there at his usual table by the window. She smiled and waved her hand, and then chose another table, where she could be alone with Kim Christopher. Seating herself and him, she enjoyed the frankly interested looks that Mr. Choe directed toward them. Nor was he the only one. Tourists, American and European, glanced at them, and she could almost hear their conversation, framed in question and conjecture. She even had a vaguely maternal pleasure in the handsome boy who sat opposite her at the small table; but he was unconscious of the looks and glances, being earnestly intent upon watching her while she used knife and fork. The table napkin confused him until he saw her unfold her own and use it on her lips. Indeed, he copied each movement she made, so resolute upon achieving correctness that she was touched.

When Mr. Choe had finished his own meal he could not contain his curiosity further, and he made occasion to pass by their table. There he paused.

"How are you today, madame?" he asked in his courteous fashion.

"Very well, thank you," she said. "I have been on a shopping expedition with Christopher."

It was the first time she had used the boy's name without the Kim surname, and she was surprised that she had done so.

A veil came over Mr. Choe's keen eyes. "Ah, yes—so," he said. "He looks very nice, almost like an American boy. You are taking him home with you to America?"

She smiled at Christopher. "Am I?"

"Please," he said under his breath.

"His mother must give her consent, must she not?" Mr. Choe inquired.

"I hope she will," she said, and was further surprised at herself. She did not think she had made any decision, but something in Mr. Choe's voice and looks compelled her so to speak.

"Ah, let us hope," Mr. Choe said gently, and went away.

The quiet certainty of his manner disturbed her, and confirmed her. When the meal was over, when Christopher had eaten a massive dish of ice cream to top off the preliminary courses, she found it difficult to let him go. Yet, what would she do with him here? Too much remained to be decided and then to be done.

"Come back tomorrow, Christopher," she told him in the lobby. She gave him the box of new clothes and lingered. "Come back tomorrow morning," she added.

"Yes, madame," he said.

She was about to say, don't call me madame, but what then should he call her? Mrs. Winters was too cold, Laura too intimate. He had his own mother, and it would only confuse him if she were to use that name. Better to leave it as it was, she thought. It would depend eventually on what was decided.

"Goodbye," she said, and refrained from the impulse to kiss his cheek.

When she returned to her room she found a long letter from Chris, the first she had received. She had been in Seoul only a few days and yet it seemed weeks, and she seized the letter, sank into a chair and forgot all else. He began:

"Dear and Only Love:

Your all too short letter—"

Yes, darling, but I hadn't anything to say yet, she murmured under her breath.

"—simply made me frantic. I would have skipped everything and taken the next flight out except that I'd have created a new problem for you. By now you've seen the boy."

Oh, I wish you'd seen him, she thought. It would make

the decision so much easier. Or would it? Perhaps it would be only more difficult if Chris saw him.

"I do hope that the woman isn't giving you trouble."

These few lines sufficed him for the problems she was facing alone. From them he plunged into an enthusiastic account of the campaign. She could see him rushing from one appointment to another, speaking on television—he was extravagantly photogenic. Her eyes hastened over the pages. Letters were pouring in by the thousands. He had tough opposition from the old guard, nevertheless. They had private detectives searching his records, examining his every act from the time he was a boy. Filthy business, but it was a cutthroat struggle. His youth helped.

"And your extraordinary beauty, my darling," she whispered.

"Henry Allen has been a rock," he wrote. "He has an unassailable position not only in the state but nationwide. Just to have his name on my masthead means everything. Of course I feel responsible about measuring up to his expectations. I must conduct an absolutely clean campaign. But that I would do anyway. I'd hate myself otherwise."

Of course, she thought proudly. She kissed the letter, folded it and tucked it into her bosom. Then she gave herself up to the luxury of thinking about him. She leaned back and closed her eyes and thought of him. In an age when love was minimized and mundane sex exalted, how had she been so fortunate as to find a man who understood love? And who can and does love a woman like me, she thought, and who wants me to be what I am and not just an appendage to him, any more than he could be just an appendage to me? So rare a happiness must not be spoiled by a boy born on the other side of the world, a boy who belonged nowhere, a chance child—oh, a lovable, lovely child, but he must not be allowed to ruin a splendid life, one that would be useful to thousands, millions of people, millions, that is, if Chris were not stopped in his career by a few enemies who were selfish entirely for their own ends and cared nothing for the morality they professed. She thought of Henry Allen with sudden dismay. Should Chris tell him, or should he not? And if not, was that entirely honorable? Oh, the frightening demands of honor!

"Darling," she wrote in her large clear handwriting. "Do you think you should tell Henry Allen about Christopher? It is so trying, isn't it, not to be just ordinary citizens, the boy our private concern, and we not having to care what people think. For of course there are thousands of children born as he has been born, and we could simply bring him home and say we'd adopted a Korean war orphan and let people think what they like. It wouldn't be their business. But now, with all your brilliant future before you, one doesn't know what to do. And I cannot allow you to give up the future, I simply cannot, because of a mistake—" she crossed out *mistake* thoroughly so that he could not see that she had written it, and substituted *an experience* and hastened on.

"It is difficult to wish he hadn't been born, for he is a beautiful boy, so like you, alas, and yet not—just himself, I suppose. I cannot make out what he thinks of his mother except he wants very much to come to you. Today I bought him new clothes—"

She had finished the letter before she realized she had written so much about Kim Christopher, five closely covered pages. She had not thought she knew so much about him. She sealed the letter and sent it airmail and then fell into a fit of such deep longing for Chris that she flung herself on the bed and wept. Not only for Chris did she weep but for home and the life she knew and loved. She saw their house, set in the quiet street just off the Square, the spacious house, faced with white marble, and inside the cool marble foyer and the marble stairs winding their way from floor to floor. Long ago a man who was an ancestor of the family of Winters had fallen in love with a lady of France, but she had refused to leave her chateau until he promised her that he would change the very heart of his American house and give it a French heart, like that of her chateau. At immense cost, the size of which increased with each generation in the telling, he had torn out the inside of his house and built it anew exactly like the house in France . . . I am homesick for the house, Laura thought, and for the tree-lined street—yes, even for the neighbors to whom she paid scant heed when she was there, for she was not a neighborly person, alas, her head always full of her own plans and her work, and at night she and Chris liked best to be alone, or at least to have guests of their own choosing.

Now, thousands of miles away, in a strange hotel in an Asian city, the house seemed a dream, except that Chris was there and she must hasten home to him again. In a few hours she could be there. He had insisted that she must keep a return ticket always with her, in her handbag, with her passport and her traveler's checks.

"One never knows," he had declared. "Don't forget that Seoul is only ninety miles or so from the borders of the enemy. You must be ready to leave at an instant's notice." She was tempted by this very instant. Yes, she could simply walk downstairs, take a taxi, go to the airfield and leave by the first jet. She imagined herself doing exactly that and at the same time knew it could not be. She was not one to run out on a job. No, she must simply think what to do next. And as though in answer to her question the telephone rang.

"Yes?" she said, receiver in hand.

"Mrs. Winters?" It was the resonant voice of Lieutenant Brown. "We wondered, Jim and I, if you'd like to take a drive and end up at Walker Hill, maybe for dinner and a couple of dances."

"I'd enjoy that," she said in desperation.

"Good," the voice rejoined. "We'll meet you in half an hour in the lobby."

"Good," she agreed.

The two men were spruce in their freshly pressed uniforms, two such very different men. "Did you know each other before you came here?" she asked irrelevantly, as Jim headed for the country.

"No, we met when Jim saved my life," Lieutenant Brown said gravely. "A mob of students was rampaging through the streets one night, in protest against the new treaty with Japan that I must say we were forcing down their throats, and I was the only American in sight, heading back to the base. At that moment Jim happened to step out of the base. He rushed into the mob and dragged me safely back through the gate. But I was beaten up."

"I'm ignorant," she said. "Why do they not want the treaty?"

"Well, it's natural," he replied. "Japan ruled them pretty roughly for more than half a century. They'd been a free people up to that time and they are proud, as you can see. The Japanese are fairly thorough themselves, whatever they do. They tried to destroy the Korean culture, made Japanese the language for schools, and so forth. The people here don't trust them—never will, maybe. They think the Japanese will get economic control again and move into total rule. Perhaps they're right. At any rate—"

She broke in. "What will happen to these half-American children?"

"Well, they'll have a rough time," Lieutenant Brown said.

"Rough!" Jim snorted. "Don't forget a lot of them have already been killed."

"Oh, no!" she cried.

"Sure," he said. "Why don't you see any teenage half-breeds around? Precious few of them! They were got rid of in the fifties, that's why. Lots of 'em, anyway. And some were castrated."

"Shut up, Jim."

"Sure they were. I know a fellow who was aide to the General who saw the kids with their little parts all—"

"I said shut up!" Lieutenant Brown shouted.

Jim maneuvered the car out of a rut and was silent.

They were all silent for a space, considering, against this superb landscape in the sunset quiet, the terrible fate of the children of war. Already the shadows lay in the valley as the sun tipped the crest of a mountain. The mountains were purple and the valleys were green. Here and there a poplar tree, golden with autumn, stood like a flaming torch against the darkness of rock and cliff. Villages clustered between the fields and now and again she saw the tall white-robed figure of a man, wearing a high hat of black horsehair tied under the chin, who was passing with dignity from one village to another, or a woman in a flowing skirt and tight bodice carrying a load on her head, her queenly figure upright under her burden. Kim Christopher! She should be grateful, perhaps, to Soonya for keeping him alive—or not grateful, perhaps!

Out of such thoughts she spoke, her voice low. "I shall never understand how our men can—can consort with these women and let children be born—"

Jim interrupted sharply, eyes fixed on the road ahead. "I have a girl, Mrs. Winters. She's a decent kid. Sticks to one guy—me. But I've told her, 'Boy, the day you come and tell me you're goin' to have a kid, that day I leave.' So she knows better. She knows I'm good to her so long as she does what I say."

"And has abortions," Lieutenant Brown said grimly.

"That's her lookout," Jim retorted.

"Some of them have eight or nine abortions a year."

"Not my business," Jim said.

Three ragged children ran into the road ahead of them so suddenly that Jim swerved the car aside and all but

struck a small wayside shrine. The children were scream-
ing at them and begging, their small filthy hands outstretched.

"Speaking of kids," Jim muttered, searching his pockets.

"They're all half-breeds," Lieutenant Brown said, peering at them.

"Villages are full of them," Jim said. "Here you are,
kids."

He tossed coins into the dust and the children fell upon
them in search, scrabbling in the brown dust and pushing
each other like dogs about a bone.

She looked at them. Yes, they were all half-American.
One small boy had red hair and freckles, and the girl had
the face of an angel, set in a frame of dusty brown hair. She
was shouting at the boys and beating them with her
clenched fists.

"Let's go," Laura said. "I've seen enough."

They had finished their dinner and were lingering over
coffee, she loath to return to the hotel room, reluctant to
be alone, uncertain what to do next. The big room at
Walker Hill was crowded with American men in uniform
and Korean girls in Western dress. She had refused to
dance, feeling disinclined to join the swaying, clutching
crowd, and Jim had whirled off with one of the hostesses, a
slim thin girl, taller than he.

"Be careful," his friend had told him. "She looks
tubercular."

"She's okay," Jim had said curtly.

"Half of them have T.B." But Jim was already swallowed up among the dancers.

"Don't they try to cure themselves?" she asked.

"They can't," he told her. "They have to keep working. Half of the children have it—at least half."

"Not that many, I hope!"

"Why not? Who cares about any of them?"

Under his dry bitterness she began to guess there was a kind man, rigid by upbringing, but rigid first of all with himself.

"I think you care about them," she said softly.

"I don't let myself."

At this moment the announcer came on the platform at the end of the room. The music stopped and the dancers paused. He smiled brightly and lifted his voice.

"We have tonight very nice treat. Belly dancer from San Francisco is here. She is very famous in America. Please watch closely her cleverness. When she is finishing, we have more treat. Miss Kim Soonya will sing by special request."

Laura started. "Did you know she was coming?"

"Certainly we did not," Lieutenant Brown said. "She does sing here sometimes, but very seldom. The last time was when we had a visit from VIPs. She's hard to get, at least that's what they say. It's considered a sort of honor—strictly on her level, that is, to get her to sing anywhere but her own place."

"Her level is not high?"

"Curiously, her personal level is high. That is, everyone knows she can't be had by a man."

"Not even a Korean?"

"No."

The belly dancer appeared, a painted blonde of striking proportions. She wore tokens of costume, a bikini strap about her loins, a gold tassel on each breast. The dancing stopped altogether, men sank into chairs and girls leaned to watch. The music blared into rhythm and the girl began her dance, an extraordinary series of muscular movements, while her body remained stationary. Her skeleton was the fixed framework upon which the flesh swelled and shrank, twisted and straightened, whirled and stiffened. Belly and breasts were independent, the belly moving like a coiled serpent and breasts, each independent of the other, swirling madly under the flying tassels. Laura, watching this physical medley, found herself convulsed with secret laughter, for above this body dance, the girl's face was a painted mask so totally without expression that it was impossible to believe it knew what went on beneath it. The blue eyes gazed unseeing upon the surrounding scene; the mouth, a vivid peony of red paint, was unchanging.

Laura looked about the room. The Americans were all laughing, but every Asian face was grave as Asian eyes were fixed somberly upon this spectacle from the West. She was aware of a creeping sense of embarrassment, mounting indeed to shame. Who was this girl? From what parentage had she sprung, and why had she not stayed in her gay native habitat, instead of wandering to these dignified and ancient shores? The dance finished, the American men burst into loud applause in which the Asians did not share, the dancer bowed abruptly and left the stage. The announcer came forward once more.

"Ladies and gentlemen, Miss Kim Soonya!"

Silence fell, and in the midst of the silence Soonya entered. She wore Korean dress, as she always did, her billowing skirt of rose brocade, her bodice silver. Her long black hair was braided down her back, and upon her feet she wore silver slippers, the toes upturned in some fashion reminiscent of her early ancestors who had come from Central Asia.

Her hands were clasped loosely in front of her as she stood, motionless, and waiting for music. It came from the small dance band, in muted chords of stringed instruments caught together by the beat of a deep-toned drum softly struck. She lifted her head after a long instant and began singing. The song she sang was not Korean. It was Tchaikovsky's "None But the Lonely Heart." There was no raucous laughter now, no staring Asian eyes. This music was universal, understood by East and West alike. In the silence her pure soprano rose and fell, melted to a whisper and lifted to a cry. When she finished there was a moment, a spellbound moment, and then a roar of applause. She bowed and left the platform, moving so smoothly that she seemed to glide rather than walk. The applause held, but she did not return. Instead the announcer came forward.

"Miss Kim Soonya thanks the audience, but she begs to be excused. She never gives encore."

Laura had listened at first with surprise, then with admiration, and finally with profound puzzlement. Why had Soonya chosen this song? And how had she learned it?

Was it meant as communication? Then communication with whom but herself? And yet how could Soonya know that she was in the audience tonight? There were too many questions to be answered, and above all was the question, what manner of woman was this Soonya?

She rose impulsively from her chair. "Excuse me," she said to the two men. "I must see Soonya immediately."

She left the hall and made her way behind the stage curtain. There in a small room she found Soonya sitting before a mirror, but she was not looking into the mirror. She had laid her head on her folded arms and was weeping in deep, half-suppressed sobs.

Laura paused at the door, then went in swiftly and put her hand on Soonya's arm.

"Soonya," she said. "It is I."

Soonya lifted her head and drew back with such suddenness that Laura was startled.

"Why you come here?" Soonya demanded. The tears were wet on her cheeks and hung on her long eyelashes.

"You sang—you sang so beautifully, but—" Laura stammered. "That song—why did you—who taught it to you?"

"Why you care?" Soonya's voice was sullen.

"I don't know, but I do, somehow." She was stammering, speaking her thoughts to Soonya before she knew what they were, but she could not stop. "We ought to understand each other, you and I. I don't want to hurt you. I hope you don't want to hurt me. Perhaps together we could decide about the boy. I haven't been thinking about you, I'm afraid, only about myself—and my—and the boy's father."

Soonya was wiping her eyes now with a delicate froth of silk which she drew from the bosom of her bodice. She rose and closed the door. Then she motioned Laura to a chair and sat down, her back now to the mirror. Biting her lip, she began to talk.

"I not brave woman. I make talk like brave. I love your—I love very much. So I learn that song for myself. It is saying what I think, what I feel. I dream too much. I dream some day he is coming back to me. I cannot love other man."

"You are trying to tell me that you want to keep the boy," Laura said.

Soonya shook her head. "No, I am not telling so. He is like father. I know now he not love me, never."

The beautiful lips were quivering and she bit them cruelly.

"Please," Laura said. "what is it you want? I will try to get it for you if I can."

Tears were flowing again but Soonya wiped them away resolutely with the silk handkerchief. "I want only money now," she said at last. "I want money for myself."

"Money," Laura echoed.

Soonya lifted her great eyes to Laura's face. "I want live alone in some house," she said. "No more House of Flowers. No more girl. No more anything. Only me, alone in house. My old servants caring for me—everything. If he not want me, then give me house alone for me."

"And Kim Christopher?"

"If no money, I keep him for my help in House of Flowers," she said simply. "If money, you take him."

"I will take him," Laura said, with instant decision.

She hesitated, about to leave, anxious to leave, and yet yearning in some strange fashion over the lonely beautiful woman. In another land, in other times, they might have been friends. What divided them was not race or language, but love, love of the same man and war instead of peace.

She put her hand on Soonya's shoulder. "I am sorry—sorry," she murmured.

But Soonya moved away. "You are lucky one," she said indifferently. "I am unlucky one."

And then as though she had not wept, or had not sent away her child, she leaned toward the mirror, and with a lipstick from an American PX but bought on the black market, she carefully corrected the outline of her lovely lips.

This, then, was what Laura had to convey somehow to Chris. The boy could not be left here. He must be taken to America.

"One step at a time, darling," she wrote that night in her hotel room. "I don't see the future clear—oh, not at all! The problem remains, what to do? But I must bring him home. The process is simple. You must send me an affidavit of paternity. I think the people at the Embassy will be kind—anyway, helpful. Declare that Kim Christopher is your son by Soonya and that I am your wife, and that you wish me to bring him back with me. I will manage the rest. If you have this document sent to me the day you get this letter, within a week I should be home. Meet me in San Francisco. Of course we'll have to pay Soonya."

She described the scene she had had with Soonya. How much money? He would know. But it would be made plain that there could be no persistent demands. Five thousand dollars, perhaps. That would give Soonya money enough to live on, lent out at interest. Or ten thousand if they must. No, it was not buying the boy. It was replacing him with the money he might have earned had he stayed with Soonya.

"Soonya wants money," she wrote, "but for a real reason. She wants to rid herself of the life she's been living. She wants to live alone. She makes me feel guilty because I am your wife, in a position she would so much wish to have for herself. I believe she loves you."

Here she paused and after an instant she inked out the last words. No, she would never understand exactly what had happened and it was wiser not to remind Chris, even now.

In The House of Flowers, Soonya was talking to Mr. Choe.

"You can see that I cannot go on forever like this," she was saying. She waved a delicate hand, signifying everything, the room, exquisite in its stark arrangements, the mats on the floor, the scroll on the wall, the single orchid in a slender vase.

Mr. Choe listened with sympathy. He was well aware of

the nuances of her life, and he knew what she meant. Before too many years her voice would lose its lovely timbre, her face would lose its smooth-cheeked beauty, and then she would no longer be an artist in her own right. She would become merely the madam of a house of prostitutes.

"I quite understand," he said.

A thought crept into his mind, not, it is true, for the first time. If Kim Soonya closed The House of Flowers and began an entirely decorous life, it would not be impossible that he would take her as his wife. People never expect a second wife to be of the stature of the first. Moreover, she had a certain distinction as an artist, a singer, a musician of some achievement, and this lent her an aura. Say what one might, the influence of the Americans had been liberalizing. When American motion picture stars, actresses and the like, were sent on goodwill tours to Asia, the Americans expected them to be received with honor. There was also the possibility now that the half-breed boy, looking so American, would be removed safely to the other side of the world. Without the boy, the clear proof that she had once had an American lover, there would be no evidence. He could take Soonya into his house without private worry. He coughed delicately behind his hand before he spoke.

"I advise that you send the child to his father," he said. "This leaves your reputation entirely clean. You have been wise to keep him hidden with your mother. I take it for granted that no one knows of his relationship to you."

"No one," she said. "He has come here only once and was then only a servant."

"Ah," he said, relieved. "Fortunately he resembles his father, not you. The coarse American blood always prevails. Send him away as soon as possible. Accept whatever is offered to you, even though it is less than you deserve for all you have suffered."

He allowed himself to look at her with a hint of tenderness in his handsome eyes as he continued.

"I have plans for you—plans for myself. There are possibilities. Once the boy is across the seas, you should forget him. You must forget all your past and think only of the future. You are very lonely. So am I."

He felt he had said enough and he rose. Soonya rose, also. She understood fully what he meant to convey, and she was grateful, though sad. Indeed, she knew that as long as she lived she would have hours of sadness. She was a warmhearted woman and while she respected Mr. Choe, she knew she could never love him. Once, long ago, a young American had wakened her womanhood, and now she was compelled, for punishment, to measure every other man against that one. In spite of reason, she had nourished hope all these years that he would come back. Now she knew he never would, for in his stead he had sent his wife, and the wife was beautiful. It was a strange golden sort of beauty, but it was beauty. She yielded to it, acknowledging its power. Her own grace, her own submissive nature, had not been enough to hold him. Perhaps American men, themselves so free, so imperious, so demanding, could love only their own strong women. Perhaps they wanted love to be a war and not a deep, enduring peace.

She did not reply to Mr. Choe but she followed him to the door, and there they parted, she bowing deeply to him again and again, and he acknowledging these bows with an inclination of his head.

III

HE WAS waiting for them at the airport in Los Angeles. She had forgotten how handsome he was—no, not forgotten, but her eyes had become accustomed, even in so short a time, to men of another countenance. She had learned to consider Mr. Choe handsome, too, and now, looking up at the tall American who was Chris, this strong, straight figure of a man, she felt the world divided into two kinds of men, two kinds of women, and between them was only Kim Christopher. No, perhaps there was also somewhat of herself. For since they had left Korea, Kim Christopher had clung to her and she had responded.

"Mother!"

He had said this word as soon as they left the airport in Korea, as soon as they had said goodbye to Soonya and Mr. Choe. Soonya had behaved entirely correctly. She had accepted a check, halfway between three and five thousand dollars, and this with scarcely a glance at it. Nor had she put it in her bosom or her purse. As though it meant nothing to her, she had left it on the table where she and Laura had last met. At the airport she had given Kim

Christopher much good advice, and in English, so that it could be understood by all.

"Obey father," she told him. "Also obey Mrs. Winters. She is father's honorable wife. Remember how I teach you all this. Rise up when father come in room. No sitting before father. Also make him happy every day your good schoolwork. In morning take tea to father always first. At eating wait he is eating. Remember all things I talk you."

She had spoken in English before Laura, to signify that she had carefully trained her son for his father, and Kim Christopher had listened, nodding, but saying nothing. Nothing did he say until the jet aircraft was high above the earth, and then he had turned to Laura with a single word.

"Mother."

She had only smiled at him, but with sudden tears in her eyes.

Now he looked up at his father. He bowed and waited for his father to speak first.

"Hello, there," Chris said.

He was embarrassed as he looked down at the slight boy—his son, indubitably. His face—impossible to deny the likeness, and his heart beat strangely fast.

"Very tall man," Kim Christopher observed amiably.

The two looked at each other. Chris did not move, but Laura took Kim Christopher's hand.

"Well, where do we go from here?" she asked, making her voice as casual as possible.

"I've taken a suite at a quiet place out of town. It's right on the beach at Laguna," Chris said. "We can talk things over. I'm taking a couple of days off to get acquainted—even with you! Your letters have been patchy. There's a lot of catching up on both sides. Things are getting hot at home. I'll have to evade reporters even out here, but I brought Berman along for that. It would be death and destruction to have bad publicity. Let's get out of here now. Berman will get your bags. Here, give me the checks."

She felt Kim Christopher's hand grow warm in hers and she released it. Chris was walking fast as he talked.

"Keep up with us, Kim Christopher," she said.

He obeyed, trotting beside her. She was accustomed to Chris's stride, but it was long and fast for a child. Chris seemed to have forgotten the boy as he led them toward the entrance. Here Berman waited for them. He put out his hand to Laura.

"Welcome home, Mrs. Winters," he said. He glanced at the boy and away again. "I'll take the baggage checks, Mr. Winters."

"Does the boy understand much English?" Chris inquired.

"No," Laura said.

"Little," Kim Christopher put in, smiling.

Impossible not to see the bravery in that smile, and Chris smiled back. "You'll learn," he said. "You'll learn quickly at school."

"School?" Laura asked.

"Explanation later," he said.

She could only wait.

Two hours later in the hotel suite he faced her. In an adjoining room Kim Christopher was asleep after a hot bath and breakfast.

"I've already made the arrangements. It's a good school," he said.

"If I had known that you would not let him come home with us," she said, "I'd have left him with his mother. He'd have had one parent, at least."

She had bathed and breakfasted, too. Now in a rose-pink negligee, she looked beautiful but not tender, he told himself. He had taken her in his arms and she had resisted him, gently but firmly.

"What have you decided about the boy?" she had asked.

Thus it had begun, this argument which might have been a quarrel except that each knew the other's love. But love must wait, she had so decreed, and he could only comply, half angry that it must be so, and yet laughing at her, too.

"I'd say you're holding out on me—damn you, sweetheart—to get your own way, whatever that is, except that I know you aren't that sort."

This he had said an hour ago when she had come from her bath fresh as a rose and had put him aside when he took her in his arms.

She had cried out in indignation. "Chris, shame on you for saying such a thing! It's just that I can't put my mind to—to—"

"To anything until you have what's on your mind settled! I know, I know."

The argument continued, and in the midst of those idyllic California surroundings which Chris thought he had so carefully chosen for the renewal of their love. They were outside now on the private deck of the suite. It opened on a small sandy beach, beyond which rolled the gentle waves of the Pacific Ocean. Sky and sea were blue, the waves touched with the barest ripple of white as they rolled toward the shore. Right and left, mountains of dark rock jutted into the sea. A proper setting, he had told himself, romantic and isolated. He had missed her horribly.

She was lying on a long chair next to his and he reached for her hand and held it.

"My dearest," he said, "if you let this child come between us—"

"He is not between us," she said. "He is simply here. What shall we do with him?"

"We are putting him in school."

"And then?"

"One thing at a time."

"All right, put him in school. Where?"

"At the Waite School in New Hampshire. It's the best of the small private schools."

"And the holidays?"

"They always have boys there over the holidays— parents in Europe and so on. And he can have extra tutoring then, to help him catch up."

"It's an orphanage," she said.

"It is not."

"He'll be an orphan, I tell you. I still wish I'd left him with Soonya. As it is—oh, Chris!"

"Darling, you feel everything too much. Think what he'd have had in Korea. No real education, no chance— nothing! He'll get the best here—"

"Except a home and his father."

He rose, suddenly angry. "All right, I give up! I'll withdraw from the race. Let's just settle down somewhere with the boy. It will have to be a strange place where I can begin again, where it won't matter."

"I can always take him back to his mother," she said.

He got up and leaned on the balustrade, gazing out over the glittering sea. Now he turned to her.

"No, you can't."

"Why not?"

"For the same reason that you went to Korea in the first place to find him. I recognize my obligation. I acknowledge that I am his father. I know that I have a duty to him. But I do not believe that my duty requires that I give up my whole life to him, all my ambitions, all that I can do if I realize that ambition. I cannot think of one person now, Laura. I could not even if he were your son and mine. You ask too much."

He was impassioned, and she responded with resolute calm.

"I am not asking anything, Chris, except to know what you will do. Now I know. But I wish I didn't. I wish I had never known about him at all. I wish you had kept your secrets to yourself."

Here she fell into silent and unexpected weeping, she who never wept, and he could not bear it. Until this moment he had not realized the enormity of what he had done so many years ago. Taken apart, it was nothing, a young man's loneliness, a young man's need, a young man—a young man.

He went to her impetuously, he took her in his arms and held her while she wept, his own heart aching.

"Forgive me, forgive me."

She lifted her head and looked at him, tears wet on her cheeks. "It's not you I'm thinking of, Chris. I understand about you. I'm not blaming you for what's past. I wouldn't think of it, because I do understand how it happened. I don't even mind. If only there hadn't been a child, I could have laughed—almost. But he's here. He'll be here between us as long as we live—wherever he is."

Her head drooped upon his shoulder. He held her long and close. There was nothing he could say, nothing. The child indeed was here.

Back in Philadelphia, the house, their home, was silent when at last they entered it, but it was midnight and silence was only to be expected. She came in alone while he paid the cab and brought in the bags, and she wandered into the living room, touching the electric light at the door. Clean and empty. Greta had kept the place dustless and neat, but there were no flowers. Chris had not told her what day they would return, for he did not know. They had not known until they left Kim Christopher at Waite this morning. Then Chris had chartered a small plane and they had flown home. She sat down now and took off her hat and gloves. This house was hers, here she belonged, and she had come back to it, but without joy. She felt strangely bereaved, or perhaps only troubled. She had not imagined that it would be so hard to leave Kim Christopher. He had somehow entered her life to stay, not as a duty any longer, but as a human being dependent upon her. Yes, she, too, could not escape the involvement; for Chris, though dutiful, was impatient to have the child settled so that he could be—not forgotten, but put into his niche.

She heard Chris close the front door and lock it. Then he came into the room.

"It's good to be home again—and have you home again. God, that a man could so miss a woman!"

He leaned to kiss her, tipping her head with her chin cupped in his hand. She returned his kiss. She knew she could not act alone. She could not bear to live without him, or live with him in anger. Nor did she know what should be done about the child. Chris had in those few days convinced her not so much by what he said as by the way he had conducted himself toward his son that only through the father and with him could the child's life be set on its right path. For after that first uneasy day, Chris had won her by his behavior. He had treated Kim Christopher without sentimentality but with warmth; and by the time they reached the school they were even laughing together over the boy's attempts to enlarge his vocabulary.

"What this, Father?"

Kim Christopher's eternal question, emphasized by a pointing forefinger, inquired of everything in sight. Food and vehicles, letters and words, objects and buildings, he had absorbed voraciously every experience of those few days. They had spent a day at Waite buying clothes, talking to the headmaster, James Bartlett, arranging for a tutor for Kim Christopher's English, and meeting Christopher's roommate, a pale blonde boy from New York whose parents were getting a divorce in Paris.

"I am impressed with the lad," Dr. Bartlett had said when they left.

This was a kind man, Laura thought, a slightly harassed man, as the headmaster of a boys' school must be, but not absentminded or abstract in his approach. If he saw a resemblance between the two Christophers he did not mention it. He accepted casually Laura's explanation that she had taken a trip to Korea, had been moved by the child's loneliness, and had brought him back to the United States with her. She added that she had told the boy to regard them as his parents. Since they had no children in the house in Philadelphia, they thought Christopher could learn English more quickly at school.

Dr. Bartlett had agreed easily. "Oh, quite. It will be only a matter of weeks. We had a boy here from Rio who spoke not a word, and you'd be surprised—"

He shouted and a smiling brown-skinned boy with startling blue eyes came forward. Dr. Bartlett rumpled his dark curly hair.

"I'm just saying how quickly you've learned English and you must help Christopher, here, not to be discouraged."

"I'll be glad to, sir," was the quick rejoinder, and he seized Christopher's arm and made off with him. A moment later they were pitching a baseball between them.

It had not been easy this morning, nevertheless, to explain to Kim Christopher. Somehow they had not been able to convey to him that school, which he had expected, was to mean their departure. When they were ready to leave he prepared to leave with them. She had then to explain.

"Kim Christopher, you stay here."

He had looked surprised, then had seized her hand and clung to it. "I go," he said.

Chris had made the next effort. "We're coming back, boy. We'll come often."

Kim Christopher transferred his hold. He took his father's hand in both his hands and in silence had pleaded, his eyes filling with tears.

"Chris," Laura breathed. "I can't take this. He's only just acquired a couple of parents, and now he's losing them. He doesn't understand. I feel responsible."

Dr. Bartlett interposed. "I advise your simply leaving. We will help him to adjust. It will take a few days, but not longer."

In the end they had, therefore, simply to leave. They had torn their hands away, he clinging to one and the other, and without looking back they had fled, leaving him to Dr. Bartlett.

Now in the empty living room, where there were no flowers, Laura, remembering, rose abruptly and went to the stairs, waiting there for Chris to put out the lights. Then, his arm about her, they mounted the stairs together.

"I wish I had looked back," she sighed.

"Now, darling," he pleaded.

"He's really very small," she said.

"Please, darling."

"I know." She heaved a great sigh. "I know, I know."

What she knew was that she had to forget, and that she never could. She must return to Chris, and she knew she never could—not with her whole heart, and what was the use of a piece of a heart? But she would do her best. Perhaps later, when he had won his race. Meantime she must return to being his wife.

Kim Christopher had seen them go without believing what he saw. He had trusted them, he belonged to them, he thought, and now they were leaving him here with strangers. It was not possible, but it was what they were doing. He saw them get into a cab, and was about to run after them except that his hand was held in a firm strong clasp from which he could not break.

"Steady, Christopher," the man said.

He did not know who the man was, although he knew his name—Dr. Bartlett. He was a tall thin man, not young, not old. He looked kind, but so had Mr. Choe looked kind. Yet Mr. Choe had disappeared from his life, as all were now disappearing. He thought of his mother, even of his old grandmother, who at the last moment had pushed him out of the house. "Go, go, go," she had said. "Go to your American father!" It was finally she who had made him glad to leave. How many times she had beaten him across his back! "You eat, eat, eat," she had screamed at him. And his mother, his beautiful mother, who would not allow him to call her his mother . . .

He had been foolish to leave that country where at least he understood what people said to him. Suddenly all his courage left him, the courage that had made him give back curses to those children in Korea who had called him Round Eyes, American, Foreigner; the courage that had made him love his mother when he knew that she could not love him, now or ever; the courage that had made him leave all he knew and come to this far country with a white woman who was his father's wife. And when he had met his father he thought that he was safe. He was not . . . he was not. He was alone again.

And here, turning around, he leaned against the tall stranger and broke into terrible weeping, great shaking sobs that split his heart into pieces. Words burst out of him, Korean words that no one could understand.

"I am lost—I am lost," he sobbed.

Dr. Bartlett stooped. It was true that he understood not one word, but into his barren childless life he accepted all children without understanding any of them very well. He simply knew that people brought their children to him, these little boys, and left them. How they could do it he did not know, but here they were, and something had to be done about them. They had to be fed and housed and taught their lessons, and he employed people to help him do this, requiring of them with the utmost strictness that they be kind and truth-telling.

"Come, come, Christopher," he said, rubbing the spiky dark hair of the sobbing boy. "They'll be back, you know. Sooner or later parents always come back. And you'll have a good time here with the other boys. Give yourself a few days and you'll be quite happy. You're hungry, I daresay. Come along and have something to eat."

It was his usual panacea for sobbing little boys, something to eat and another boy or two to sit with them and talk and play jacks, or something like that. He had a good housekeeper, Mrs. Battle, who was enormously good at making things boys liked to eat, and he led Kim Christopher to the big kitchen. There she sat, drinking a cup of tea.

"Here's a new boy, Mrs. Battle," he said. "He needs cheering up. The usual thing, except that he doesn't speak much English. He's come all the way from Korea. Mr. and Mrs. Winters brought him. They live in Philadelphia but he's to stay with us. There's a story in it somewhere, but which one of the boys doesn't have a story? Well, anyway, I suspect he's hungry. Christopher, his name is."

"Lucky I've just made sugar cookies," she said. "Leave him to me, Dr. Bartlett."

She drew a chair to the table and poured another cup of tea and put cookies on a plate. "Sit down, Christopher."

He sat down, rubbing his cheeks dry with his fists, and she smiled at him while Dr. Bartlett tiptoed away. They sat there, then, the two of them, saying nothing to each other, for what was there to say, she thought, if the poor child could speak no English? She put a cookie on his plate and then another when he had finished it. The tea was hot and strong and he seemed to like it, poor child. His tears ceased, he became quiet and at last relaxed and even sleepy.

She rose. "Come lie here on the settee, lovey," she said. She patted an old couch, its springs worn from her own weight. "Lie down here and let Mrs. Battle cover you up. Take a little nap and you'll feel ever so much better when you wake."

He understood what she meant if not what she said, and

he lay down and let her cover him with an old knitted afghan of many colors. In a few minutes he fell asleep, worn out with travel and sorrow.

Far away in The House of Flowers, Soonya was superintending the packing of her possessions. Her departure was quiet but absolute. Mr. Choe had been entirely correct. The change had been made through a friend of his, a Mr. Joshua Pak, a wealthy businessman, who was now increasing his assets by privately cancelling his contracts with Americans and substituting for them new contracts with Japanese firms under the terms set by recent trade treaties with Japan. He disliked Americans who were righteous and could not be corrupted, and he despised Americans who could be corrupted. Korea was full of both kinds. With the Japanese there was never any question of corruption one way or the other. Business was the only consideration. Mr. Pak was filled with secret fury, moreover, because the stupid young Americans in the armed forces had spawned so many half-breed children. Korean girls were in it for business reasons, but the men were spendthrifts and fools. He advocated in safe places that such children be strangled at birth, or if they lived that at least the boys be castrated. The blood of Koreans was ancient and pure, and it was intolerable that it would not remain so. Through the centuries they had not mingled even with Chinese or Japanese. Why then should this present miscegenation take place?

Exchanging confidences with Mr. Choe, he had said boldly, "Such children must be taken away from our country, even though it is only to cast them into the sea."

Mr. Choe was not so severe. He had been softened somewhat by his years in America, but he too agreed that the children should be sent to the land of their fathers, for they belonged there. Americans knew nothing of purity of race. Behold their many colors in skin and hair and eyes! Mr. Choe had also taken the occasion before he asked a favor of his friend to say that he himself had been instrumental in returning a half-American boy to his father in the United States, the mother being one of the women in The House of Flowers. He had then proceeded to ask his friend the favor of being the go-between for himself and Kim Soonya. Mr. Pak had agreed since Mr. Choe's factories turned out certain products which he wished to contract for, and favor deserved favor.

Hence, on this fine autumn morning an American limousine waited outside at the gate. Inside her room Soonya was gathering her last possessions. There remained the private drawer in her dressing table which she kept always locked. Sending her maid from the room now, she unlocked it and took out the pictures of the father of her child. Gazing into his handsome face she had a vague stir at her heart. She had lied to Mr. Choe in telling him that she had no love for the American, and there were times when she believed her lie. Now, however, she knew her own heart. Were they together once more, a dream she had at last relinquished, she would have loved him again. This man was her love and there would be no other. Between them, even before they could understand each other's language, there had been a flow of feeling. He had loved her; she would always believe that he had. His wife was second in his heart. Soonya was compelled to believe that also. Otherwise she could not now proceed to Mr. Choe's house, which she must do, for the years were passing and she was at her height, professionally. In a year or two she would begin to show her age, and another younger and more beautiful woman would take her place. But as the wife of Mr. Choe, though only a second wife, she would have position as long as she lived. She gazed for an instant more at the handsome pictured face. No, she must keep no photographs, not in another man's house. She hesitated only for one more moment, then lit the candle that stood in its lacquered stand on her table, and holding the pictures in the flame she watched them kindle and curl and turn to ash.

One more picture remained—that of the child, three or four weeks old. She had held him in her arms, and he, the father, had taken the photograph. As she studied it, it was upon her own face that she gazed. How young she was, and yes, how beautiful! The child, too, had been perfect, and dressed in American clothes. He had bought them somewhere and brought them with him one day, and she had put them on the child and together they had posed for the picture in the tiny rock garden of the small house he rented. The child had grown and changed, and now it seemed to her that this baby whom she had tenderly loved was not the boy, thin and foreign-looking, who had gone away with the American wife. Somewhere along the way she had ceased to love the child. Perhaps, unable to hate the father, she had visited her hatred upon the child he had left behind him. To the father she had felt close, his flesh and hers united; but the child was a stranger, an interloper for whom there was no place. She held this snapshot also to the flame. Then, sighing, she swept the ash into the palm of her hand, and rising, she went to the shoji that opened into the garden. Lifting her hand, she blew the ash away and watched it drift through the air to settle on moss and rock and to float upon the surface of the pool.

And she knew as she did so that her memories could not be so easily swept away. Deep within herself was the knowledge that she had taken a stranger into her most secret being, a man from a foreign land who remained a foreigner and who would never return. But she had had him in her, and that part of him which she had received had taken on a life of its own in the form of a child. Henceforth, however great the distance between man and woman, the child lived as a permanent record of their union. Nothing could destroy that child. Even his death could not destroy him, for he had lived and would live, though he died, for what had been once could be again, would be again, in the lives of other men and women. Nothing was inviolate where men and women were concerned. The child, moreover, carried in himself disparate halves and in his lifetime he would impart disparity to other children yet to be born.

Such thoughts were in Soonya's mind. She was a woman neither simple nor stupid. She was capable of deep feeling, out of which these thoughts arose like birds skimming the surface of the sea. She put them away, however, and looked about to see that nothing was left in this room that had belonged to her. Then, seeing there was nothing, she summoned her maid and they went out of The House of Flowers and entered the waiting limousine and were driven away.

"Mistress," the maid at her side whispered. "Are you not afraid?"

"Afraid of what?" Soonya asked.

"To live in the house of Mr. Choe, and such a big house as I hear it is?"

"Certainly I am not afraid," Soonya replied. "I am beginning a new life."

In her heart, however, she was afraid, for she never had been a wife, and now she must be one, whether she liked it or not.

"What's your letter?" Chris asked.

They were at breakfast on this summer's day. Greta was setting glasses of orange juice before them, and the fragrance of bacon and coffee hung upon the soft morning air.

"It's Wilton, from the laboratory," she said. "He wants me to come back full time, to supervise his researchers in the algae project. He's especially interested in Euglena."

Chris laughed. "Euglena—at least I know it's not a girl!"

She smiled. "Not a girl, but interesting for all that. It's the green stuff one sees on a pond of fresh water in warm weather—an autotroph."

She lifted her eyebrows, waiting for his question. Earlier in their married life he would have asked it, interested as he was in her work, proud of it then.

"No, I'm not asking what that is," he replied to her expression.

"Then I'll tell you anyway," she said. "It's a plant that needs nourishment the way an animal does. Instead of giving out vitamins as plants usually do, vitamins have to be given to them. Euglena, for example, needs Vitamin B_{12}."

"So?" he said.

"So Euglena research may help us find answers to questions about human anemia or even leukemia."

But he was not listening, she could see. He was thinking his own thoughts.

"I wish you wouldn't go back to the laboratory just yet," he said.

"But what shall I do with myself, Chris?"

"Be decorative for a bit—as my wife! I've got to do active campaigning. I need my beautiful wife at my side."

"I'm not good at handshaking. You know that."

"I'll do the handshaking. You just stand near me and smile. Remember your model technique! It was devastating."

"So long ago!"

"Only a couple of years. Before you got to be Dr. Laura de Witt, Ph.D. in all this scientific stuff!"

"You've been patient."

"I've been proud. It isn't every governor who has a double-barrelled wife. Beauty and brains!"

She took up another letter, and recognized the handwriting. "We have a letter from Christopher. He's beginning to write amazingly well."

"What has he to say?"

"It's to you, as usual. Shall I—"

He nodded. She opened it and read it aloud:

"Dear Father: I am writing you today. Now I can swim and dive. Also play baseball and so forth. Now the boys are going home for summer. When am I going home, please? Shall you tell me? Few boys will be here soon. I am hoping I see you every day. Perhaps you will come. I have good marks. Your son, Christopher."

"Nice kid," Chris said.

They seldom spoke of the boy. What was there to say? Neither had the answer to the question that remained in the heart of each of them. She knew that Chris thought of the boy, if not constantly, then often. He was here, a living presence in their house, however far away he was.

"Will you answer the letter, Chris?"

"You answer it."

"What about the summer?"

"I inquired about that when I chose the school. There's a summer session—sort of a camp. A good many of the boys don't go home—parents divided or traveling—that sort of thing. Military officers whose wives go with them, but they have the children where it's safe and they can go to school."

She put the letter into its envelope. "One of these days he will not accept my excuses for you. How can he understand that you are too busy ever to write to him?"

"Please, Laura!"

She looked up, startled by the anguish in his voice, and immediately softened. "Chris, forgive me. It's just that we did bring him here, you know. He's in a strange country, among strange people."

"We'll go and spend Christmas with him."

"O Chris, will you?"

"Why not? Besides, you wouldn't be happy just with me. We're not two any more."

"Only because—"

"I know, I know. It's my fault."

"I wasn't going to say that. Only because he's so alone. If you'd decided to leave him with Soonya, I'd have put him out of my mind."

"Well, I would not have! Letting him grow up in that goddamned country—"

"It's Soonya's country."

"Shall we send him back?"

"If you say so, Chris. I'll take him back."

He put down his knife and fork. "You really mean that!"

"Yes, I do. He must have someone near him, Chris, someone who loves him."

"Laura, you exasperate me. He's getting an education, he's fed, he's housed. He's growing up in a country of opportunity. He can be anything he wishes to be. I'll see that he gets the best."

"Everything except what he needs most—a home."

He flung down his napkin. "All right! I give up. I'll tell Berman I'm withdrawing. We'll spend the rest of our lives taking care of this boy."

"That would be final. So final that I would see a divorce in the offing."

"Laura!"

"You wouldn't be fit to live with."

"I can't say I enjoy this life."

"Meaning me?"

They had quarreled before but never like this. She looked into his eyes, bright blue with anger, and felt her heart chill. How could she explain that there was a trouble now which went deeper than the matter of the boy; explain that the real agony was the intolerable doubt that he might not be quite the man she had thought he was; that he might evade the truth instead of facing it, take less responsibility than full manliness required, a fall of pride in him she could not bear?

Not fair of me, she told herself. I'm measuring him by my own demand. If the boy were mine, would I acknowledge him if it meant giving up what I hold most dear? But with her, "most dear" could mean only Chris. If she had had a child born out of wedlock, for example, a child she had left in an orphanage, and if she had felt sure that Chris could not accept the child, would she have told him? Or kept silent forever? No answer to this, for there was no such child. And for Chris now the loss was not of a person but of his highest ambition. Nor was the ambition only for himself, she knew. He was too well born for that, too beautifully educated. From the old Quaker stock he had inherited the tradition of service. He wanted power, yes, but he wanted to be a good governor because the people had the right to honesty and devotion in their administrators. His every waking hour since he grew up, since he'd finished law school, had been concentrated on planning reforms and improvements for the state. Try them out in the state, he had said, and so find out what would work one day for the nation. He never added the words, "when I am President," but they were there in the silence and they both knew it. Only last night he had got out of bed and prowled about the room, then had waked her to listen to his latest idea for tax reform.

She listened, admiring the resonant voice, the blazing eyes, the words matched to thought in strong, persuasive speech.

"I do so believe in you, Chris," she had said. He had come to her then, had taken her in his arms, and in the torrent of their mutual love, it had been dawn before they slept.

Yet now, only a few hours later, they were quarreling. She loved him none the less, and yet she knew a flaw had been revealed. He had not told her of Soonya. That she could forgive, but he had not told her of the boy, and that, somehow, she could not forgive. For the boy was innocently born. By no will of his own he had been called into life, and whatever the means, he had the right now to live, and not a hidden, secret, shameful life, but a life in freedom of spirit. Yes, there was a loss, but she could not lay her hand upon it. Chris simply did not stand quite as tall as once he stood, and this in spite of love. But he was all she had.

"Chris, forgive me! I love you so."

He melted at once. "God knows I love *you!* There's nothing in my life but you, no one! I want everything for you, sweetheart! I want you to be proud of me."

Two steps and he had her in his arms.

"Excuse *me!*" A voice at the door and they sprang apart. Berman stood there, his face flushing. "I'm sorry to interrupt a love scene, especially between a husband and wife —a rare sight these days."

Chris laughed and stepped back. "But quite legal! Come in, Joe. Pour him a cup of coffee, Laura. As a matter of fact—" he sat down again at the head of the table, and she took her place decorously opposite, "—matter of fact, Joe, we were just about to decide how my wife could help in the campaign. Sit down."

Berman sat down between them. "That's what I came to see you about, Mr. Winters. We've got the women organized now—clubs and so on—and they all want to hear you, Mrs. Winters. I'll book you as close as you'll let me, beginning with the local groups here in the city and then fanning out over the state."

She was startled. "They want to hear Chris, not me, and what shall I talk about?"

Berman smiled at her. "We must save him for the men, so what are you interested in?"

Chris broke into fresh laughter. "Don't ask her that! She's interested in the oddest creatures—deep-sea things— plants that are animals and animals that are plants. Women will think she's drunk, but they'll listen."

Berman looked puzzled. "You're kidding."

Laura came to his rescue. "What I am is a marine pharmacologist. Don't let Chris tease you, Mr. Berman."

"But you were a model, I thought."

"That, too. That's how I earned my first money after college."

"Stick to being a model, honey," Chris said joyously. "It's becoming. Don't be scared, Berman."

"I'm not," Berman protested. "You can talk to the university women about your scientific side, Mrs. Winters, and to the others about being a model."

"Where do I come in?" Chris inquired.

"Oh, you'll come in everywhere she goes. The women will want to know what sort of husband you make, whether you help with the dishes at night and whether you like children—"

He broke off.

"It's been a great disappointment that we haven't had children," Laura said quietly, unperturbed. He was not to think it made any difference.

"She can do it," Chris said. "Book her up, Joe. We must get the women started. Did you arrange for me to speak at the National Rotary?"

"All set."

She rose from her seat quietly, so quietly that they did not notice that she had left the room. Outside, summer was coming into bloom in the walled garden. There was a precious quality to a city garden. In this small space she had planted carefully a few graceful shrubs, a corner of rose bushes, a mimosa tree fringing the wall between their house and the next. A fountain, two white iron seats and a round table between completed the living picture she had made. Strange how she kept remembering the landscape of Korea, the wide stretches of bare mountains looming above the streets of Seoul, the curving roofs of the palaces, the crowds, the children's faces, the faces of the special children—the ones like Kim Christopher, the ones her eyes had learned so soon to search for and to find.

She sat down on one of the iron seats. A bird sang suddenly out of the sycamore tree that leaned over the brick wall, one of the double row which grew along the quiet street, but she scarcely heard, her mind far away. Today the life in that ancient city of Seoul, the old strong life of the past, the people of Korea, was meeting, head-on, the new life, the fierce alien life of young American men. And now, unexpectedly, the face of Lieutenant Brown floated up out of her memory.

A tense face, she recalled, tense with the decency of self-repression, the control of his sexual instincts exhausting him as much, and perhaps more profoundly than, license. Who knew? How could she blame her Chris, her mercurial, loving, gay Chris, whom she could not have loved so passionately had he been like Lieutenant Brown? How could she blame him for falling in love, even for a while and not forever, with so beautiful a girl as Soonya?

She heard the front door shut, with a bang as Chris always shut it, and knew that Berman was gone. She rose then and went in to him and reached up and clasped her arms around his neck.

"I will help you all I can," she said.

A light summer rain, the aftermath of a thunderstorm, was falling as she got out of a cab and walked into the lobby of The Towers. She was growing used to it now, this meeting of women in their chosen haunts, today in the huge apartment of Mrs. Henry Allen. She was not afraid any more, and scarcely shy. She liked old Henry Allen for himself as well as for what he was doing for Chris. She felt him a rock of strength for Chris; and for herself, too, a friend whom she could trust, though she told him nothing. He liked her and treated her with a courtesy, tender and delicate, that he might have accorded his daughter, had he had one. Six sons he had begotten, but no daughter, and though he was loyal to the wives of his sons, he missed a daughter. She was at ease with him, feeling in his bulk a depth of understanding which perhaps she had felt with no one else, certainly not with her own father, a college professor of the old school, kindly, forgetful of his children, whose interest in literature ended with the Elizabethan Age. There was comfort, too, in Henry Allen's rectitude. No danger here of an old man's furtive caresses!

She entered the elevator and mounted to the eighteenth floor. The door opened and Henry Allen stood there to welcome her.

"Come in, Laura," he said. "They're all here—all the old guard, the bankers' wives, the wives of hereditary Quakers like me, the hoarders of gold. They won't part with a penny unless they have to, and we must see to it that they have to, you know. You must make them see how a new conservative, dynamic and intelligent man like Chris can save their country from the things that scare them— from all the things they call creeping Communism. You'll know how to do it. They'll open their hearts, and their purses, to the young rightists of whom Chris is such a superior, such a forward-looking representative. The old lady under the purple tower of a hat—she could underwrite the whole campaign dinner here if she would. I want her to do it so that I can put my pittance into tours for Chris—a swing around the state, the farmers and all that —every county seat, you know—and then maybe a trip around the world to give him background. Every man needs that, these days."

She followed him into the opulent drawing room where upon small gold chairs were seated a hundred expectant ladies. She met their appraising eyes with calm, smiling just enough but not too much. Yes, the modeling helped her very much. Stance, aloofness, poise, presence, she used them all with practiced grace. And she knew her women. She must not rouse their jealousy by being too sure of herself. She must approach them with young, appealing modesty, she must be willing to talk about herself only as the wife of a rising politician, she must be ready at the end of her short speech, for she knew better than to talk long, to leave time for questions, for she had learned to make her points there. Mrs. Allen rose to introduce her, a stout kindly figure in gray silk.

"We women always want to know what a candidate's wife is like, don't we? And it is not often that one is so pleasant to introduce as the one we have with us today, Mrs. Chris Winters. You've seen her picture many times in our papers, for she's a busy young woman, accompanying her husband everywhere. But for most of us this is the first time we have seen her as she is, by herself."

Diplomatically she omitted all reference to the model,

Laura de Witt. There was something not quite solid about glamour.

"And so, here she is, our future first lady."

Laura rose, smiling shyly, and it was not a simulated shyness. "I am only pretending to be used to this sort of thing," she said. "The truth is that I'm not used to it at all. I live quietly. We both do, actually, and I'm here only because my husband has asked me to come here for him, since he is engaged elsewhere. So I am merely taking his place. He'd have so enjoyed being here if he could have. I scarcely know how to begin—perhaps by introducing him to you. What's he like? Well, he's six feet two and he has blue eyes that grow very bright and shining when he is interested in what he's talking about or when he's just angry. He plays a cracking game of tennis and he's an excellent skier and a good horseman. We both like to ride. He likes golf but I don't. He went to Harvard and was graduated with honors in economics. His first job was in a big New York bank, where he stayed until he felt that he understood money, how to use it, how to take care of it, how to lease it as credit to business houses. And then he went back to Harvard to take a degree in law. He completed his military obligation in Korea and after that, well, he belongs to an old law firm here in the city. That's the outside of him. At home he's—"

She hesitated, her head bent thoughtfully. Then she looked up and smiled at them. "How can I tell you what he's like at home? We have no children. We wish we had. He'd make a good father, I'm sure. He's strong on discipline—conservative, logical, but fair. He's always fair."

She paused again. There rose before her, out of the atmosphere, the image of Kim Christopher. No, no, she must not think of him now. She faltered and then went on quickly. "Politically, he represents the best of the Young Republicans—or so I think, and a good many other people do, too."

She went on, artful in her artlessness, and she knew the women were meeting her with warmth. She was honest, she wanted to be completely honest, and wished she could tell them about Kim Christopher, yet knew she had no right to tell what Chris himself would not. She ended her talk soon, and then met their questions with patience and some admiration. For the questions revealed that these women were astute, sheltered though their lives had been. They knew their city and their state, and when the time came for them to expand their knowledge of their nation and of the world, they would learn. Somehow she remembered here a story her father had told her long ago when he had come back from a year of study in China.

"Those Chinese peasants," he had said. "They can't read or write, but they are civilized and sophisticated. Only a few years ago they were used to no more than wheelbarrows and mule carts as modes of travel. Then the first railroads were built and with ease and total aplomb they climbed on trains with their produce in baskets hung on bamboo poles. Now they're getting airplanes, and without amazement or hesitation, they step aboard, as I saw an old fellow do, with half a dozen chickens tied together by their legs. Up in the air we went and he smoked his brass-bowled bamboo pipe and gazed out of the window as though he'd been riding aircraft all his life. And my interpreter told me it was his first trip on anything faster than a donkey. Even the railroad had never come to his part of China."

She could imagine these plump, white-haired, and well-dressed ladies, whose world was the comfortable, opulent city in which they had been born and lived, stepping into the world over which Chris hoped to preside with the same sort of acceptance.

"And that," she said, in conclusion, an hour later, "brings me to the end of the afternoon. I've enjoyed it so much. I've learned from your questions—and thank you."

She turned and was about to sit down when Mrs. Allen put her hand on her arm. "Wait a minute, my dear, I want to introduce you again. Friends, I introduced you to Mrs. Christopher Winters, wife of our next governor—oh, yes, I'm sure of that, dear—but now I want to introduce you to another young woman. This is also Dr. Laura de Witt, the distinguished young scientist, who is working with two of our very greatest scientists in the field of marine pharmacology. And if you don't know what that is, don't feel embarrassed, because I didn't know, either. I had to look it up. It has to do with finding new medicines from plants and animals in the sea. Is that right, my dear?"

It was Laura who was embarrassed, but the ladies clapped their hands warmly and rose to find tea and cocktails. No one asked her what marine pharmacology really was, and she avoided the subject skillfully while she balanced a teacup on her knee and ate a caviar sandwich.

She paused an instant at the door, however, when she

was taking leave. "How could you?" she murmured reproachfully to Mrs. Allen. "I'm afraid they won't like me now."

"My dear," Mrs. Allen said resolutely, "it's time we women were proud of women who have brains."

With this she kissed Laura's cheek, opened the door and let her go.

"Dear Father," Kim Christopher wrote. "Next week is coming July Four. Big Day and fathers are coming, also mothers. I am hearing so. Please come to see rokit. Your loving son, Christopher Winters."

She handed the letter to Chris in silence. He read it. "Did this come today?"

"Yes. Shall I mix you a cocktail?"

"Please. Of course we can't go on the Fourth. I'm making that big speech in the state capital. That's the night of the hundred-dollar dinner. You must be there with me. What's 'rokit'?"

"Rockets, of course—fireworks."

"Oh, yes. Too bad, but, well, I said we'd go for Christmas."

"Here's your cocktail." Christmas is a long time from July for any child, she thought. But she was used to this now, or so she told herself. The campaign was in full swing and she admired Chris with heart and mind, smothering the small intolerable doubt in frantic activity. He was making one brilliant speech after the other. People were expecting more and more of him. "A man of courage," they called him. He was facing unsolved issues, searching for answers to the great questions, studying, learning about the countries even as far away as Asia, where most of the real problems were rising. No one knew, including Chris himself, how desperately she wished he would face the unsolved private issues too, and reassure her miserable soul that he was indeed a man of courage. Nagging at her memory was the story of Grover Cleveland, who, running for the Presidency, had said "Tell the truth" about the unfortunate boy he'd been supporting for years. Was Chris less of a man than Grover Cleveland? It was worth her life that he should not be . . . and worth his, too.

"Sometime after Election Day I shall have to take a trip around the world," Chris was saying. "Maybe during the Christmas holidays. That's a dead space. You and I."

"But not over Christmas. We'll be with Kim Christopher then."

"We will. I said so."

Her mind was plotting while he talked. There were ten days before the Fourth. Dr. Wilton had begged her to come to the laboratory to look at a new marine microorganism he had been able to grow in his experimental tanks.

"I need your sharp eyes and quick mind," he wrote. "The little beast—beast?—is a real self-propelling eater. At the same time it—vegetable?—contains chlorophyll, and it photosynthesizes. It may be a new screening device for anticancer agents—I hope and pray!"

"Chris," she said now, over their cocktails, "shall you mind if I take a day off now and go up to the laboratories? Wilton thinks he's really found something new."

"Of course not," he said with such quick generosity that she withheld her second question. And do you mind, she was about to ask, if I delay a day or so longer and go to see Christopher, since we can't go on the Fourth? No, leave that unspoken. Perhaps when she was in the laboratory, bent over a microscope, it would not seem so urgent.

"Thank you, Chris," she said.

"A small return," he replied. "Very small indeed. Henry Allen said you bowled the women over the other day. They liked you, sweetheart. They've more brains than I gave them credit for."

He came to her side and leaned over her and kissed her long and deeply. It was still exciting.

A week later she spent two days in the laboratory, enjoying, after so many months, the delight of communion with minds like her own. She was more pleased because under the microscope she had been able to recognize the new organism as one of the dinoflagellates which she had once seen but had not analyzed in a mass of plankton from the Sargasso Sea.

"Your relentless brain," Dr. Wilton had grumbled. "Of course you'd remember you had seen the damned thing— probably in your babyhood! Don't you ever forget?"

He was older than she, a slim spectacled man of no particular coloring, but rather a male man, she suspected, and so she merely smiled. Driving herself early the next morning along the parkway toward New Hampshire, however, it occurred to her that one of her difficulties perhaps was that indeed she never did forget. Thus she was unable to forget a single moment of the hours she had spent with Kim Christopher, nor could she forget the changing looks upon his too expressive face, his disappointment when he found that he was not to be with his father, his brave silence and the glitter of tears in his eyes. No, her absorption in her work these last two days had not made her forget the boy's urgent need. And, not forgetting, she had for the first time in her life consciously and wilfully deceived Chris.

"Chris," she had said last night over the telephone. "I shan't come home tomorrow as I had planned. I am staying on another two or three days."

"You'll be late for the Fourth!" he exclaimed.

"No, I shan't be. I'll get in not a moment later than the midnight of the third, possibly the second."

"And be worn out the next day!"

"Not worn out the next day."

He had yielded to her inexorable good humor and they had parted with the usual words of love.

How right her decision had been was clear to her now after the long quiet day of driving alone. She had finished her task at the laboratories, leaving with her colleagues a brief clear statement of her conclusions, and with peace in her mind, the peace that only completed work, well done, could bring her, she had turned her inner attention to the matter of Kim Christopher. Slowly as the hours passed she had come to the conclusion that the situation could no longer be allowed to hang fire. The boy must either join them as Chris's son, or she would take him back to Korea and his mother, that is, if she could so persuade Chris. Her mind quieted by at least this much decision, she drew in at sunset to the grounds of The Waite School for Boys. She had purposely not announced her coming. She wanted to see Christopher as he was, without the preliminary excitement of expecting her arrival. She wanted to come upon him wherever he happened to be, at play or at his evening meal. She stopped at the main building, a colonial structure of white-painted wood with green shutters at the windows, and rang the bell. An older boy answered it.

"Is Dr. Bartlett here?" she asked.

"He's still in his office, I think, but he's just about to go home, probably."

"Catch him for me, please," she said. "Tell him it is Mrs. Chris Winters."

She had lingered in the hall only a moment when she saw Dr. Bartlett loping toward her, his long stride hastened by the surprise evident on his face.

"Mrs. Winters!" he cried. "Is something wrong?"

"No," she explained, "simply that I thought I'd drop by and see how Christopher is doing."

"Very well, very well," he said. "Come in. I'll send for him."

"May I just go to him wherever he is? I'd like to see him on the spot, so to speak."

They found him in the library, otherwise empty at this hour. There on a window seat, catching the last of the evening light, he was reading a large book upon the sill.

"Christopher, here is a surprise for you," the headmaster said.

He looked up. She saw at once that he was thin, much

thinner than he had been. But when he leaped to his feet she saw also that he was much taller.

"You come to see me!" he breathed.

To her horror he hesitated, and then, leaning his head against her shoulder he began to weep. She put her arms around him and held him and turned a reproachful look upon the surprised Dr. Bartlett.

"Has he been unhappy?"

The boy answered for himself. He lifted his head and smiled through the tears wet on his face. "I am happy now," he said. "You come to see me. Thank you."

"He's been happy," Dr. Bartlett said. "Of course there has been some depression. After all, it's a strange country for him, and in a manner you and Mr. Winters are still strangers to him."

They had not told him who the boy was, and though it must have been evident to the eyes of a wise headmaster, no questions had been asked and so no answers were necessary. Should she tell him the truth later, when they were alone? He was still talking.

"You mustn't take these tears too seriously, Mrs. Winters. I've been several times in Asia and indeed spent months in Japan during the Occupation, and I remember that it is not thought a disgrace in Asia for a man to weep. Rather, it is considered a sign of sensitivity and feeling. Our Christopher has both these attributes, I have discovered. Of course he has problems, perhaps."

"We'll discuss it," she said with resolution. "Meanwhile, can you put me up for the night?"

"Of course, in our best guest room. Christopher, suppose you take her to the East Room and then you may bring her to dinner with you. I'll have your bag brought in, Mrs. Winters. Now I'll leave you with your boy. After all, it is he you came to visit."

He left them, and she was touched that Christopher did not feel himself too old to clasp her hand as they went down the hall, noisy with crowding boys. Turning eastward down a corridor, he opened a door and followed her into the room, a pleasant place, she observed, all chintz and white organdy. She sat down in a cushioned chair and, putting out her hand, she drew the boy to her side.

"Now let me see you," she said. "You are tall, you are thin. Do you eat enough?"

He nodded, suddenly shy. To her surprise she saw his eyes fill again with tears. She said nothing, comprehending the inner tension, the insecurity, which kept tears so near the surface. But this must not go on, she thought.

"When is coming my father?" he asked.

"He is coming," she said with determined cheerfulness. "And certainly we will come for Christmas. You know Christmas?"

He nodded.

"Yes, Christmas," she repeated. "Now tell me—" An idea sprang into her mind. She released his hand and motioned to a nearby chair. "Do you know how to ski?"

"I know what is," he said, seating himself. "But I don't know how is."

"Then you must learn," she said. "Your father is a fine skier. It's his favorite sport. When we come at Christmas time there will be snow on the ground and he will want to take you skiing on the mountain yonder. The boys here all know how to ski, I am sure. And you will be a good skier, like your father. Will that make you happy?"

He nodded again, his eyes growing bright, and she was cheered.

She went on, "I'll see that you get a good ski teacher, and we'll leave word for your skis and things."

"You skiing, too?" he asked.

"Yes, but not so well as your father does."

In such chatter they continued, and within the hour a gong sounded for dinner and they went into the dining hall. And then suddenly, at the table, seeing Christopher at another table, talking with other boys and eating with fair zest, she decided that she would not reveal the secret Chris wanted hidden. For how could she explain? Her loyalty to him came first.

She went with Christopher that night to a school play, a comedy of school life acted by the boys, and parted from him later at the door. Remembering how often he had laughed, she had bade him an easy goodnight.

"We'll have breakfast together," she said, "and then I must go back to your father."

The brightness faded from his face. "Goodnight, Mother," he said, and giving a little bow he left her. She watched him walk down the corridor and when she could see him no longer, she closed the door.

"I simply felt I had to see the boy and discover for myself whether he is happy—happy enough, that is, so that my conscience can rest, temporarily at least, for we haven't solved anything. You know that, Chris!" It was the next day. She had reached home late, nearly at midnight, and Chris had waited for her in the living room, surrounded by newspapers. Now, bathed and in her rose-silk negligée and further refreshed by a cool drink Chris brought her, they were sitting on the upstairs balcony on long chairs in the moonlight.

"I don't know what to make of your going off like that by yourself," he said, troubled, as she could discern from the timbre of his voice. "You might have had an accident on the road and I would not have had the slightest idea where to find you. You probably didn't leave word even at the laboratory. No, I know you didn't, for Dr. Wilton called here this morning, wanting to get in touch with you. If he had called last night, before you called me, I'd have been sick with fear. Such things happen these days, Laura, and you've no right!"

"I know I should have told you I was going, but somehow I had to get off by myself. I had to see him."

"Why?"

"I couldn't forget him."

"Can you now?"

"Not altogether, not until we answer the basic question of what we are going to do with him."

He gave a great sigh. "If only he didn't look like me!"

"He does look like you. And sooner or later the truth will catch up with us. It will and it should."

"Later, when I've won my race—"

"Later it will be worse. The Governor? A scandal! President? The scandal of the century! Chris, you can't have your cake and eat it too. You can't keep this boy on ice forever. You've got to decide sometime whether fame's worth more to you than a son." And oh, if it is, she said to herself in silent agony, you're a lesser man than I thought you were. You can't mean what you say about human values and live this kind of a lie.

He was stung. "That's not the choice," he retorted. "Of course I want a son. I always have." He did not see her wince and he went on, not knowing how relentlessly. "Under ordinary circumstances, if I were an ordinary man, I'd take the son—*this* son—and declare my fatherhood to the world. Fame? I don't give that for it." He snapped his fingers. "Any fool can have it nowadays. Take off your clothes, you've got it." He turned and stared at her for a moment, and she could see the anger rising. "Is it possible that you, my own wife, can't understand me?"

"You want power, Chris," she said softly, "of course you do, and you'll use it well. I know that better than anyone. You'll enjoy power, too. And there's nothing wrong with that either. It's just that—"

"Laura!" He waved his hand impatiently. "Do I have to spell it out for you, of all people? I want to be governor of this state because I want to be a good governor for the people of the state. Not for my own sake, but because I see wrongs that I feel I know how to right. If possible, and I intend to make it possible, I shall one day be the President of the United States, and not for the fame of that, either, but because I see wrongs in the nation that I believe I know how to right. Humbly I say it, and I shall need the help of many people—beginning with you, Laura." The sharp note reappeared, and she found it hard to bear, then faded into a moment's silence before he went on in a voice husky with intensity. "I believe in myself. I know my motives are good. I want to leave the mark of greatness on my times—yes, and I will. Because I have, I think, found some remedies, some solutions. Now, I repeat, am I to throw all this away, throw myself away, throw away all I can do for the country, because I made a mistake when I was a boy in Korea?"

He swung his long legs around and sat sideways in his deck chair, searching for Laura's eyes in the moonlight. But she held her face in her hands and kept her gaze averted. She trembled as that wonderful voice went on, still husky with feeling, but speaking now to her and to her alone.

"I had thought I was going to die, Laura. That shakes you loose from your background. And I was surrounded by human misery. You were a world and a lifetime away. Desperately I needed someone to be close, to—some simple, happy human warmth. In this I was no different from all the other young Americans, only I tried to keep away from all the cheap females who hung around the others. If I had not met Soonya, I would have stayed lonely. She was lonely, too. And though I met her at that dance hall, she was no cheap bar girl. From what you say, she still isn't, in spite of how she makes her living. You saw her quality yourself. She loved me, Laura, and needed me as I needed her." He was almost whispering now. "And it was not cheaply that I felt about Soonya. It was all very young, very rootless, shallow, irresponsible. But it was not cheap. It was nothing, nothing at all, compared to my feelings about you." She nodded, mutely. This she had been sure of from the beginning, and had all along found it comforting. But she could not yet look at him, the turmoil in her heart overwhelming her.

"Well, so a child was born. It was the last thing I wanted. I felt terrible about it. I felt frightened and guilty. I admit there was a moment when I felt the wonder of having begotten a son. Yet I never thought of him as really mine. I never dreamed of bringing him here. He was born in Korea, he belonged in Korea. And then I thought— maybe I was just easing my sense of guilt—that it was a good thing that Soonya now had someone of her own to care about, because I was about to leave her and come home."

For a long moment neither of them spoke. Then Chris said quietly: "This is a wicked thing to ask another woman to understand, my Laura. It's why I couldn't tell you when I first came home. And I loved you so, my extraordinary wife with such beauty and intelligence and gentleness beyond anyone's, that the Korean girl and her child faded into unreality. I had promised her nothing, we had given equally to each other, the past was past. And when I thought of her child at all, I thought of him as all hers. How could I know that she thought of him as mine, that according to Korean law he belonged to me?

"But our people would never understand all this in a man who wants to be governor—and someday President of the United States. People are cruel. I know how cruel they can be and how unjust. Am I to throw away the whole usefulness of my life by inviting their cruelty and injustice? I do not intend to put myself in their power. I do not intend to ruin life for myself, for then my life would also be ruined for them. Vanity? It's not. It's dedication."

She was listening to him now. But he was, she knew, speaking no longer to her alone. He was making his case before some tribunal she could not see, the people, the nation, the world, or life itself. She understood and did not reply, could not have replied. Instead she rose and went to him and, kneeling beside him, she laid her head upon his breast. Under her cheek she felt his heart beating hard and strong.

The months slipped past in a kaleidoscope of brilliant days and nights, and hours of weariness so exhausting that she felt sometimes as though she were in a strange land, among strange people whose language she could not speak. Her face felt stiff with smiling, her hand was sore with grasping the hundreds of hands outstretched to her, and her slender body grew fragile as she lost weight from sheer fatigue. It was a life apart from life. She and Chris were actors, acrobats, performers. She had to have new clothes, a constant change of gowns and frocks, for photographs made a garment obsolete in an evening, in a day. But Chris showed no sign of fatigue. He was exhilarated, upheld by exaltation, a sense of mission. While he strove to convince people that he was destined to be their leader and their governor, he also convinced himself the more thoroughly that no other man could serve as well.

The times were troubled. World tensions, the war in southeast Asia, the strife between rising nations stirred tensions here at home. Tension was a fire consuming the nations, Laura thought. A burst of flame in a far place brought flickers of fire everywhere, creeping tongues of fire in dark places to burst out in fresh conflagration.

"Chris," she sighed at night. "The times are evil. I wish we had not been born in this age."

"Nonsense," he said robustly. "It's the most exciting age there's ever been."

"Tremendous possibilities," she agreed, "but too large an *if—if* people do this, *if* people do that—"

"I don't intend to leave it to people," he declared. "I intend to lead them. Step by step . . . to where I want them to be."

"Lead them where?"

"We've had all we need of splinter groups, unions, brotherhoods, national groups, racial groups, everyone disaffected! They've forgotten to be Americans. To hell with the nation, as long as we get our benefits! You watch—" he shook his finger at her with a cheerful grin. "Once I am in the seat of power you'll see a benevolent dictator!"

"Berman won't like it if you say that in public," she smiled.

"There's a time to speak and a time not to speak, and I shan't be such a fool as to speak out of time. I'll maintain the principles of patriotism now and make the definitions later when I've won my battle."

What they all feared as the last days drew near was the gossip that might be taking place underground, where they could not combat it. Laura drew from somewhere in her compendious memory a story that her father had told of President Harding, and how his enemies had concocted the tale of his having Negro blood. Two generations ago, and yet prejudice was as virulent today, about mixed blood of any sort, as it had ever been. True, Harding had been elected, but under a shadow—whether of truth or of untruth. And Grover Cleveland, acknowledging his illegitimate son, had also been elected. But the gossip about Chris, if it existed, would pack double dynamite, exploding both prejudices at once. Her anxiety now fully aroused, she refused to allow herself to visit Kim Christopher again, and sent him only unsigned postcards lest some zealous reporter make the connection between them.

As the autumn days drew on toward November, as the first frost fell and the trees turned red and gold and then ashen while their leaves fluttered in the chill winds, she became aware of a grim change in Chris. He was with Joe Berman from noon to dawn. Her fears finally burst into speech.

"Chris, is something going wrong?"

"No," he said shortly. "It's just the machine. I'd made up my mind to ignore it and then to fight it. But I am faced with the fact that if I want to be elected, I have to work *with* it. And the further it goes the uglier it gets."

"What does Berman say?"

"What he has said from the beginning—patronage jobs, contracts to the right men. People are lining up for the big final dinner, a thousand dollars a plate minimum, and those who give more have their hands out already for the top jobs. Somehow I thought I wouldn't have to capitulate." He shrugged uncomfortably. "But I do. And I'm too angry to quit. Meantime, you know what a fine-tooth combing I get—my religion, morals, college escapades, business deals, campaign costs—everything is under a microscope, the evil pursuing eye of a political enemy! This country is decent only during a full-scale war. Do you want to stir up a big one for me, Laura?" He laughed grimly. "I've spent over a million dollars on this election, and they can't discover a penny that isn't my own. Now they're raising a stink because they say it's undemocratic to spend one's own money—limits government to the rich! That's because my honorable opponent came up out of poverty, whereas I am more lucky. Well, I'll do what I must until election is over. Only a few more weeks to go!"

They had not in weeks mentioned Kim Christopher and they did not now.

Dr. Bartlett was in his office, studying the report cards about to be sent to parents the next week. He knew each of the one hundred and fifty boys in his school, and he kept watch over the progress of each. Now he heard a knock at the closed door.

"Come in," he called.

The door opened and Kim Christopher stood there. It was near the end of the day and the headmaster had planned to leave the office early, for it was his wife's birthday and he had a gift which he had not yet presented. A boy always came first, nevertheless, and especially this one.

"Sit down, Christopher," he said.

Kim Christopher sat down carefully on the edge of the straight chair on the other side of the desk. "Please, sir, do I trouble you?" he asked.

His English was improving so fast that in another term there would be no difficulty. Dr. Bartlett was beginning to believe that this slender boy, now growing too rapidly, would be one of his rare ones.

"No trouble at all, Christopher," he said cheerfully. He shuffled the reports he had already seen. "I've just examined your marks. Excellent! I'm very pleased. Still a little trouble with history and English, but your mathematics make up for it."

"I like mathematics. I am coming here today to ask if next term I may take some science," Christopher said.

Dr. Bartlett lifted his eyebrows. "Usually we postpone that until your second year."

"I like science very much."

"What science?"

"Physics, please."

Dr. Bartlett leaned back in his chair. "How old are you?"

"Twelve years, sir."

"Have you had a birthday since you came?"

"Yes, sir, last week."

"You didn't tell anyone?"

"No, sir."

"Now that was a mistake. We always like to know birthdays, and Mrs. Battle makes a cake. Promise me that next time you will tell. Here, I'll just take down the date."

"October twenty-six."

Neither of them spoke of any family remembrance, but each was aware of the omission. Kim Christopher was silent for a moment, unwilling to leave, and yet hesitant to stay.

"Well, Christopher?" Dr. Bartlett said kindly.

"May I talk something more, sir?"

"Anything, my boy."

"About myself."

"What about yourself?"

Kim Christopher lifted his eyebrows. "Who I am, please?"

The headmaster looked at him quizzically. "You are one of my boys."

Christopher was patient. "For myself, who I am, sir?"

The headmaster rubbed his chin. How was he to reply? "You tell me who you are, Christopher."

"I don't know, sir. I think I am my father's son, name is Winters, as you know. But now I am not sure. Maybe I am only mother's son, name is Kim."

"Where is your mother, Christopher?"

He was treading unfamiliar ground, forbidden, perhaps, but where a boy was concerned no one else came first.

"She is in Korea, sir. She is Korean woman."

"Tell me about her."

Kim Christopher flushed. "I am knowing too little. For me she is my mother, very beautiful face. I have also Korean grandmother, very old and not so nice, often angry with me for eating much food, and so on. But my mother is not so. She is quiet, but sometimes—"

He shook his head and stopped. Dr. Bartlett prodded him gently. "Sometimes, what?"

Christopher looked away. "She hates me for something."

"Surely not," Dr. Bartlett said, perceiving a wound, very deep.

"She hates me," Christopher repeated. "I think it is for some reason because I am American, like my father. In Korea I am American. But here I am not sure. It seems here I am Korean. There I am called Round Eyes. Here I am called Slant Eyes."

"Who calls you that?" Dr. Bartlett demanded. This at least he could stop.

"Some boy. It is all right. It doesn't too much matter. Only I like to know what I am, wherever."

The headmaster felt a familiar stab in the region of his heart. How often a boy came here to this room with a private pain! It was not easy to be a boy, facing his own manhood with despair or puzzlement. And this boy's bewilderment had a special twist. How could he explain to Christopher what he was? His own thoughts were not clear and he must feel his way.

"You are interested in science, Christopher, so let me explain it in those terms, in terms at least of biology. Let me tell you about some valuable and interesting creatures in natural science. They are the new species, the connecting links, between the kingdoms. When they are in a vegetable environment—you understand environment?"

"Yes, sir, I have looked that word in the dictionary."

"Good. Well, in a vegetable environment they function as vegetables, but in an animal environment they become animal. Mrs. Winters is an expert, I'm told, on such creatures. Have you talked about your interest in science with her? No? Well, at any rate, these creatures are a connecting link between the kingdoms of creation. Or, speaking of environments, let me take the dragonfly. You know the dragonfly?"

"Many in Korea, sir."

"Here also. Well, they begin life in the water. I suppose they think—if they think—that they are water creatures. But one day they feel the urge to rise to the surface of the water. There they shed their skins and suddenly they find themselves with wings. They have never known wings before, but as soon as they have them, they soar away into the sunshine, never to return to their water beginnings. What I am trying to say is that all through nature we have these valuable links between the kingdoms, between the species and now between the races. I call them valuable because they make a unity of creation. Divisions are not permanent."

"You are meaning me, sir?"

"Yes. Someday there will be so many like you everywhere in the world that no one will call you names. It is a process of nature and it cannot be stopped. You are important. You are essential. I cannot tell you how you happen to be born one of these link people, because I don't know your story. But someday you will know. Meanwhile, remember that you are valuable and that you have been born for a purpose—nature's eternal purpose, first to diversify and then to unify, and so make of life a continuing, continuous stream."

Long words, which the boy could not possibly understand, he thought, and yet he would not explain. Let the young mind stretch and reach through its own puzzling! Kim Christopher was looking at him with large and thoughtful eyes—beautiful eyes, it suddenly occurred to him. He rose.

"And now I must get home, Christopher, for my wife has a birthday and I like to have dinner with her."

Kim Christopher rose also, and bowing, he left the room.

At the dinner table that night, after Dr. Bartlett had presented his gift of an antique brooch, he told the story of Kim Christopher. Mrs. Bartlett sat at her end of the table and listened, the brooch fastened at her neck. Sometimes he forgot her birthday, in which case she never mentioned it, his devotion being the atmosphere in which she lived, so that a birthday forgotten had no significance. Nevertheless, it was pleasant when he did remember, and never more pleasant than this evening. She listened, therefore, with more than her usual interest.

"Of course it's perfectly clear who the boy is," she said with decision, which was her habit. "Chris Winters is certainly his father, and it happened during the Korean War, and, well, that's it. Why the boy turns up in this country just now, I wouldn't know, but why he is here with us, well, it's perfectly plain. He came at a most embarrassing time. A man who is running for governor in his state can't suddenly produce a half-Asian son, can he?"

Dr. Bartlett looked at her, thinking aloud. "And just when can such a man produce such a child?"

"That's the difficulty," she agreed. "There is no suitable time. If Winters is elected, well, how does a governor unveil to the public a son twelve years old? If he loses—I don't know—I don't think he'll lose. He's making quite a swath nationally. He's a brilliant orator and papers all over the country pick up his speeches."

Dr. Bartlett was grave. "What's to become of this boy?"

"Hard to tell," Mrs. Bartlett said cheerfully. She poured fresh coffee. "He can't live hidden forever, that's sure."

In his own room Kim Christopher was considering carefully his own situation, dividing the favorable and unfavorable aspects. He had plenty to eat, he liked school, he had friends, he wore good clothes, he enjoyed sports, he had kind teachers and he could and did worship the headmaster, who, he wished, was his father. It would have been his good fortune to come to this strange country and find such a father. As it was, his feelings about his true father were mixed. He was drawn to the tall man who was still young, and yet he felt held off from him. Did he wish to return to his mother in Korea? No, for she too held him away from her. His memory of childhood was made up of her sudden bursts of affection and her equally sudden and inexplicable moods of hatred and even cruelty. Here at least no one slapped him or bade him be gone. If he was not wanted, exactly, at least he did not feel unwanted. As for his father's wife, whom he liked to call Mother but who never called him her son, he did not know where she belonged in his life. She was always kind, but she too seemed not entirely his own. Moreover, what part had he in their lives, when he did not know where they lived and could not reach them except through letters? Now there were not even letters. He lived in a sort of twilight. The simile occurred to him as he watched the sun set over the distant mountains and the darkness descend.

As that same sun set behind Rittenhouse Square, Laura settled gratefully in front of the fire with a book. It was one of those rare moments when campaign pressures let up enough to allow her to indulge her private pleasure. She flipped to page 218 where she had left her marker. Her constant preoccupation with the problem of Kim Christopher's life, yet to be solved, had driven her, for her own relief if not for a solution, to the works of the anthropologists. This one was *Man's Most Dangerous Myth, The Fallacy of Race*.

"In this connection," Ashley Montagu wrote, "it has been said that one cannot get out of a mixture more than one puts into it. This is one of those facile generalizations which are too easily allowed to pass by the uncritical. When we combine oxygen and hydrogen, we obtain water . . . When we combine zinc and copper, we obtain an alloy, bronze, which has far greater strength, and numerous other qualities, than the unalloyed metals comprising it; that is certainly getting more out of a mixture than was put into it. When two pure bred varieties of plants or animals unite to produce offspring, the latter often show many more desirable qualities and characters than the stock from which they were derived. Surely the varieties which man presents in his various ethnic forms would suggest that something more has been produced out of the mixture of the elements than was originally brought into association."

She put down her book suddenly, aware all at once of something she should have been aware of months ago. Though this child, a hybrid, was the first who had presented himself to her, surely history was full of them, as men swarmed over the earth and met women of other peoples. Now for the first time it occurred to her, she realized with shame, to think of Christopher in terms of his own potentials. Until now he had been an adjunct of Chris, someone to be fitted somehow into their joint lives, hers and his. What if Chris had unwittingly produced a human being important in his own right?

This idea immediately assumed such proportions in her imagination that she felt a fresh rush of guilt. What if this child were indeed a treasure? What if he had a mission to fulfill in the future, when she and Chris were old and useless? If so, what were they doing to prepare the child for that future, Chris having endowed him with the double life of American fatherhood and Asian motherhood? She saw now that Kim Christopher, in human terms, might be more important than Chris himself could be, even though Chris became the President of the United States; and this in biological terms as well as human. Her scientific mind, so unnecessary in a woman, she sometimes thought these days as she followed Chris from city to city, sprang into action and began regarding Kim Christopher as a new kind of responsibility, exciting but overwhelming. The production of any child was an enormous responsibility, the creation of a new life to be burdened with living out a lifetime in joy and sorrow, but to create Kim Christopher was beyond what she had yet perceived. He was a step into a future of which she and Chris were totally ignorant. Oh, he must not be left to live out his youth in a boy's school!

"No, indeed," she said aloud, although she was alone in the library. "No, indeed, Chris, it is not enough to feed him and shelter him and see that he gets an education. Far, far more must be done for him."

But when could she speak such words to Chris? Not, certainly, at this moment. There must be no repetition of her July outburst. Election day was only a few days away, now, and all was going well. Chris's transparent honesty, his single-minded dedication combined with his good looks and resonant voice, enchanted his listeners, as she could very well see. And Joe Berman was beginning to breathe more easily. As yet there had not been the briefest wind of gossip about Kim Christopher.

"We'll make it," Joe had said the other day as they waited for Chris after one of his great climactic speeches. "I was mortally afraid at first that some skunk would smell out—you know what—but I guess we're safe. You got to be careful though. I leave it to you now, Mrs. Winters."

"I can't be sure of preventing gossip. I'm not even sure of people in our own offices. The bills—"

"You pay the school bills yourself, don't you?"

"Yes, I do take care of all such details myself, but you forget that at the school no one knows the truth, or is in any way on guard. It would be quite natural for someone up there to speak to someone else of a child in whom we have a special interest."

"It mustn't happen," Berman said doggedly.

She looked at him, a political boss of the sort that she tried not to despise, and yet a man who, she knew, was utterly devoted to Chris. It was one of Chris's talents to win the love of men as well as women. She was used now to hearing a woman declare, "he's the most attractive man I've ever seen"; but it was different and more rare to know that a man like Joe Berman, crass and crude and all but dishonest, would and did sacrifice himself for Chris. It was distasteful, too, in an inexplicable way, and she could not refrain now from expressing the distaste by contradicting him.

"All the same, you know, it must come out someday. There's no such thing as hiding a secret forever—not for a man like Chris. And how can he bear it himself, to wake up every day thinking—"

"That's his talent," Berman broke in, "*not* to think if he don't want to. He wakes up in the morning knowing what he has to do that day and he shuts out all the rest. It's a gift. He don't agonize."

Joe was right, of course. She was the agonizer, not Chris. So was she, after all, perhaps, the one who would have to solve the problem of Kim Christopher? Ah, she wished that she had not begun thinking of him just now in this new and urgent way! He was always there at the threshold of her mind, but she must learn to keep the door shut. As it was, she saw him there, always waiting.

In that corner of his room which was his own, Kim Christopher was engaged in a private activity. There had been few hours of pure, absorbing play in his life. His place, he had learned in Seoul as one of the "new people," was always on the fringe of the crowd and in games he had been the spectator, the one pushed aside if he came near the center. Here in this school where he now lived, a place which he had at first thought was an orphanage for boys, until he discovered that parents came to see the other boys and that at vacation time boys went away to return again, he enjoyed to the full the games in which he was encouraged to take part. At first he could not believe he too might—nay, must—run after a ball, that he, too, could throw and catch. He was quiet by nature and by the habit to which he had been compelled through years of rejection, but now he learned to shout and call. In the daytime he busied himself with his fellows, and was on the whole accepted by them. In the evening, however, in this hour between sports and dinner, which was his own, he worked with his puppets.

Now, the door shut and his roommate, John Barstow, somewhere else with other friends, Kim Christopher drew aside the curtain which hung over a large dry-goods box, and revealed to himself a small stage upon which stood three puppets, which he had carved out of cherry wood. One was his Korean mother. The other two were his father and his father's wife, that woman whom he wished to think of as his mother, and yet could not, for reasons he did not know. He took from a cloth a fourth figure, a boy, dressed in American clothes. This figure he was also carving from cherry wood, as he had carved the others. The Korean mother was dressed in Korean garments, the other two in Western dress. The boy's figure was still far from finished, and he opened the small, sharp pen knife which was his tool and went to work, perfecting the head.

He could not remember when he first began to love puppets. There were not many puppet shows in Seoul, for people preferred to go to motion pictures and such modern entertainments, but he had known one old man who had been born in Seoul, and who had made puppets and performed with them for forty years and more, or so he said one day when Kim Christopher, pressing close to watch him carve the figure of an old country woman, had asked questions.

"Forty years and more," the old man had mused, "though no one wants to see the plays nowadays, not even the great ancient puppet play, *Gogdu Gagsi Noreum.*"

"I want to see it," Kim Christopher had said in a firm voice.

The old man had pushed his spectacles to his forehead and then had smiled at him.

"You shall see it," he said, "for I am to perform it tomorrow night at the Buddhist temple, at least part of it, for it is long and there are many parts to it."

Sooner or later Kim Christopher had seen all the parts of this long play, made up as it is of six different stories, with the result that even while he was in Korea he had begun to dream of making a puppet play of his own. He had neither material nor tools then, and so it had remained only a dream. Here, however, he was allowed to carve his figures in art class, and though he had not explained to his teacher the story of his play, for it was only beginning to grow in his own mind, his teacher encouraged him to carve. His favorite story in the old play in Seoul was when the hero, a lowly man and lonely, Yeongno, makes fun of a nobleman, a yangban. Kim Christopher had no wish to make fun of anyone, and yet he had always felt a sympathy with Yeongno, and thought of himself as such a person, one who could not find his place.

Tonight, therefore, he worked with great care and industry upon the figure of himself. He did not as yet know how the story he was weaving about these four characters in his own life would come to an end. Indeed, he saw no end, and therefore could not tell what would happen to this small wooden figure upon which he worked with such absorption. In the midst of it the bell rang for dinner, the door opened and his roommate entered. They did not speak, but John came near and stood at his shoulder.

"That's neat," he exclaimed. "It looks like you."

"It is me," Kim Christopher said, offhandedly.

"Then who's those?"

"My father—my mother."

"Who's that?"

"I have two mothers."

"You can't have two mothers. Nobody has."

Kim Christopher did not answer. He could not explain.

"Can they?" John persisted.

"In Korea, yes," Kim Christopher said.

He closed the knife and wrapped the wooden boy in a linen handerchief, laid him down and drew the curtain across the stage. There was a feeling of comfort in making the puppets which he could not explain. But the story troubled him. How could the story end, when it seemed there was no end?

"One thing at a time," Chris said.

They were in his bedroom, he and Laura, she looking very beautiful in a white satin evening gown. White belonged to her, he thought fondly, seeing her in the mirror before which he stood to arrange the bow of his tie. She was slim, her red-gold hair flaming, her slate-gray eyes dark, and she carried herself with a delicate pride, a glamour which always reached his heart. And yet he knew that inside the brilliant accidental beauty was another woman, a grave quiet woman, one with simple tastes and a deeply thoughtful mind.

He had made the remark in answer to her question, "Do you sometimes think of little Christopher?"

The truth was, as the far from stupid Berman had observed, that he did not like to think, not, at least, in the sense that she did. Where she could not help pondering, he postponed thought with impatience, trusting to intuition. All day he put aside decisions, then in the night, before sleep, he faced the decisions that he must make before the next day. He would, as it were, empty his mind and wait for an impulse to appear which felt right to him. It was the one he chose. But he never let an impulse about

Christopher appear, lest it crystallize into premature action.

"One thing at a time," he repeated.

The bow was tied to his satisfaction—he hated ready-made bow ties—and he reached for his dinner jacket.

"At what point," Laura persisted, "shall you let the boy's future be settled?"

She knew she should not ask him, that he was not ready to answer. But her new sense of the child's significance and her need to talk to Chris about it were too much for her. So now as they prepared for the great dinner, the thousand-dollar-a-plate dinner, she put her question.

"I don't know," he said. "One doesn't decide these *whens*. I'll know when the moment comes. Then I'll see in a flash what I should do."

In a flash it would be, yes, she sighed. She had only hoped the time for the flash might have come. But nothing she could do would hurry it. She knew how his mind worked, and that no decision was ever as sudden or as impulsive as it seemed. Again and again she had seen how a question would thrust itself upon him, as she was sure this one had, and then be pushed aside, but each time he would give it a passing glance of increasing familiarity until, apparently upon the moment, he would decide. He was impatient with her long reasoning approach, he would have no involved logic. He had a genius all his own, living at the top of his bent, listening to everyone, picking brains everywhere, accumulating information, letting decision follow. And his conclusions were so nearly always right that she trusted him. So let her trust him now!

She would see his intuitive gift at work tonight, she was sure. She doubted that he yet had any clear idea of what he would say to the crowd of his supporters and friends, but when he rose to his feet, when he faced them, searching them, he would draw upon them for inspiration, and then, out of the well of his own feeling and knowledge he would give them that for which they waited, that which they drew from him, that which they craved. And he would tell nothing but the truth. It was his genius to seem—nay, to be—every man's friend, but when his mind defined conclusion, it would be his own. She knew that he would be a good governor. She believed that someday he would be a great President.

An hour later, from her seat at the head table with Chris the brilliant host, she surveyed the flower-laden, overcrowded ballroom. To her right was Henry Allen, looking, she thought, somewhat fatigued.

"How will it go?" she asked.

"He has it in the palm of his hand," the old man replied. "And time, too. I don't think I could stand another day—or night—of campaigning. Yet nothing seems to tire him. Look at him—as fresh as a boy! He can't be stopped."

Could he be stopped? A whispered word, a question asked at the wrong moment, in the wrong place, and could he be saved? If only Kim Christopher had been brought out of the shadows, into the light where truth could disarm slander! She was conscious of an immense inner strain, and she sat quietly, watching the crowd, listening to the bursts of music. Berman, too, was anxious, or so she imagined. He sat near Chris, serious and silent, yet nervously quick to notice any commotion at the doors. Tonight if an enemy rose to his feet the whole structure, so carefully built by so many people over these past weeks, could fall into a heap of dust, and millions of dollars could not put it together again. Her imagination, always too quick to conjure disaster, saw Chris downfallen, all his bright spirit gone. How could life go on in such a case?

"You're very thoughtful tonight, my dear," Henry Allen said.

"Yes," she said, "an occasion like this makes one thoughtful, doesn't it? So much responsibility—"

"He can take it. Someone says—I don't remember where I saw it—that genius is the infinite capacity to make use of everyone and everything. Our man has it. I don't mean that in any derogatory sense, either. He simply draws life toward him and he feeds upon it, and is fed upon by others. It's a sort of spiritual photosynthesis."

"I dread to think what will happen if he doesn't win."

She realized on the instant that this was not wholly true. If Chris went back to being a private citizen, Kim Christopher could come home. But how could Chris be an ordinary man when he was never ordinary?

"He will win the governorship," Henry Allen was saying with energy. "Surely you don't doubt it?"

"Something can always happen." She longed to tell him what she feared.

"Nothing that he can't surmount. The people are solidly behind him. He's made a magnificent job of campaigning. I don't believe there's a single county in the state that he hasn't visited at least three times. He's met every issue fully and evaded nothing. The people trust him because they know where he stands. He's the only man who can stand up against the present governor."

He paused for reflection and then went on. "Do you know, watching him as he works, I see that Chris has the technique of a creative artist. No, it's more than a technique. It's his basic quality. Very modern, too, not at all in the classical tradition! An artist begins his picture, or a writer his book, without any notion of what he's going to paint, or write, but the plan grows out of the material he has, and there's a creation. That's the way Chris works, with people and with ideas. They're around, he sees them, understands them, uses them—and somehow creates an order where before there was none."

They were interrupted by Berman, who left his seat and came to whisper in Henry Allen's ear.

"Time for you to introduce the candidate, Mr. Allen! I've given you ten minutes."

Henry Allen stood up. "I won't take that long."

"Take it, take it," Berman whispered. "Lead up to a big climax. The people are waiting for it."

Across the vast space of the ballroom, people were moving their chairs and waiters were hurrying to clear the tables of dishes. The light of twenty-four chandeliers glowed upon the many colors of women's gowns and jewels, sparkling against the somber black and white of men's evening clothes. The band was playing softly, and now, as Henry Allen came to the rostrum, it broke into a march, then subsided. In the silence his high, clear voice reached to the far corners of the room.

"It is my privilege tonight to tell you the story of a man,

a man born in our own community, of a family famous in our state and our city, a man born and educated in the traditions of our people."

It was, she perceived as he went on, a masterly speech. Henry Allen began quietly, his voice literal and unemotional, eminently reasonable and calm. But as he proceeded, he introduced a subtle fire, a pervading power of emotion based upon logic and fact. He touched upon the incidents of Chris's childhood, upon his youth, his distinguished career at Harvard and then as a young lawyer in their city. Impeccable, high-minded, brilliant, good friend and good fellow, the character of Chris emerged strong and sympathetic, capable and idealistic, a man able to make dreams come true.

"And so I present to you," Henry Allen concluded, "this honorable man, Christopher Winters. He has served us well here in our city, and now he asks to serve in wider spheres."

He stood aside, and Chris came forward, debonair and confident, modest and proud. Applause rocked the chandeliers and roared through the huge room. He waited, smiling his famous smile, and then began, his voice firm and melodious, his delivery confident and practiced.

"My friends—"

And listening, her heart straining, Laura knew this would be his greatest speech.

Far in the night they sat together, a handful of waiting people in Chris's downtown office, as the votes came in from headquarters. By dawn it became clear that Chris would win. Out of five and a half million votes he had won by seventy-five thousand.

"Congratulations, Governor!" Berman's voice was husky.

"Congratulations—congratulations—"

They crowded about him and he smiled at them, half bewildered. He was exhausted, as Laura could see, but triumphant, and he grasped the hands outstretched to him, the hands of people who had stood by him, of people who had worked for him, his office staff, his campaigners. Standing aside, waiting, she allowed them their reward. Then quietly she went to him and kissed his cheek.

"You'll make a great governor," she said.

The moon was veiled, or it had set, she did not know which, or perhaps it was even the dark of the moon, when at last she lay upon her bed in her own bedroom. It seemed long since she had had time to observe the moon, whose light she had always felt conducive to the sort of mood and meditation in which she did some of her most reflective thinking. Lying in this very bed, before or after love, or in those pauses when Chris was too employed to think of love, she had gazed often on the moon as it hung outside the wide window which faced her bed. Tonight, after the excitement of victory, Chris had suddenly yielded to exhaustion. None could have guessed, and for once she herself was deceived by the heartiness of his manner, his joyousness properly combined with a decent modesty, as he received congratulations. Reporters had descended when his victory was confirmed, and from them at last

Chris had laughingly, apologetically, extricated himself, crying, "Tomorrow, fellows—no, I don't really know how I feel about it. I'll have to find out—" and so saying, had led her by the arm and they had escaped and come home. Then, the door once closed and locked, he had crumpled and she caught him before he fell.

"No, no," he protested, "nothing's wrong. Everything is right. I'm not beaten, but beat."

They had come upstairs, and she had laid out his night things while he showered, and then she had seen him to bed and the windows opened, and by then he was already asleep. So she had left him, sunk in slumber, and had closed the door between their rooms, so that no movement of hers could disturb him. For she was sleepless. Now that the race was won, what would they do with victory? She bathed in leisurely fashion, she brushed her hair, she went to bed at last and lay in the unlit darkness and remembered what Henry Allen had said, that Chris was an artist, and worked as an artist works, with his material and from it, waiting for its own shape to take form.

She must wait, too, leave things as they were—yes, wait if need be until after Christmas. When Chris was with Kim Christopher, when the three of them were together, he would from this fresh experience, this new material, know what he must do, what they must do, for her life was his. With this thought, peace fell upon her and in its quiet she slept.

"He has adjusted very well," Dr. Bartlett said.

They were waiting in the school sitting room for Kim

Christopher to appear. Christmas holidays had begun the day before. Most of the boys were gone and the building was quiet. Outside the snow was falling in windless silence, great drifting flakes of white against the winter gray.

"He is probably working with his puppets," Dr. Bartlett said.

"Puppets?" Laura inquired.

"He is quite talented," Dr. Bartlett said. "I wish he could be equally diligent in all subjects, but we must not ask too much. He has learned a great deal in a few months."

"Do the boys like him?" Chris asked.

"The ones whom he likes do like him very much. The others seem to—respect him. He carries himself well. By the way—not by the way at all—his English is excellent. He's good in languages. And he has a fine singing voice. The music master has put him in the choir. He seems to enjoy that."

"What about sports?" Chris asked.

"He's not for heavy sports like football. He'll take to tennis, I should think, and he does well enough in baseball. He is lacking in a sense of competition, which is rather a handicap, since we use games to develop the competitive spirit so essential in our society. He enjoys doing something well without seeming to care if he wins."

They were interrupted here by the entrance of Kim Christopher—"Or," as Laura had said, on the way here today, "let's just call him Christopher, without the Kim. Don't you think it's time?"

"As you say," Chris had replied absently. He was driving and they had talked very little as the hours passed, and scarcely at all about the boy. Let it be seen first what he had become, they had seemed to agree. They saw at once that he had become another than the boy they left. Even Laura saw that, although she had seen him since Chris had. He came to the open door and stood there an instant. He was taller, much taller, that they saw. He wore a dark blue suit with long trousers, and this added to his height and to his age. He was clearly more than a few months older. That they saw. What made him really older was a new gravity, not quite sadness, a perceptive acceptance, perhaps, that no longer allowed for the ready smile, the lighting eye of childhood.

They did not speak to him, Dr. Bartlett with intent, for he wanted the boy to make his own approach to the two who somehow belonged to him and to whom he belonged, a relationship which the headmaster thought he understood but still found puzzling. The boy said "my father," but he did not say it as easily now as he had when he first came. Nor did he write to the man as often as he had in the beginning. Indeed, checking with the master of his dormitory, he learned that the boy had written no letters for many weeks and had received only postcards. Nothing had yet been explained.

Laura did not speak. She had made up her mind on the long, almost silent, journey today that Chris must make the direct approach. Son and father must solve the problem of their relationship. She could only be a bystander. She sat quietly now in her chair, gloves in hand, her mink jacket across her knees, and waited, allowing herself no more than a welcoming smile.

Christopher looked at her uncertainly, smiled briefly, and then fixed his grave eyes upon his father's face. He had been expecting them all day, since no one knew when they would arrive, and all day he had not left his room except for meals. He had not been idle, however. Throughout the day he had been carving his new puppet, a small boy with a round face and Korean features. The wood was hard, as was the material of the other puppets, and since it was his last piece he had carved slowly and with care. Once his knife had slipped and cut his thumb. He had bandaged it himself with a strip of white cloth.

Chris looked at the headmaster and then at Laura, as though he expected them to speak. Then, seeing them silent, he spoke with a gruff heartiness.

"Hello, Christopher. Come in, boy!"

He held out his hand and Christopher came in. They shook hands, and Chris did not let the boy's hand go for an instant. "You've grown tall," he said.

"Every day I eat meat," Christopher explained. He withdrew his hand gently and sat down on a chair at the other side of the room. There he was silent, but easily, as though he were deferring to adults, as indeed he was, remembering Soonya's admonishment that he was never to speak first to his father, but remain silent unless he were asked a question, and then he must speak clearly and with as few words as possible, waiting for his father to proceed.

"That's good," Chris said. "A growing boy should eat meat every day, eh, Dr. Bartlett?"

"We think so," the headmaster said, smiling.

It was now his turn and he spoke kindly to his pupil, and quite without condescension. "I've just told your father and Mrs. Winters that you have shown remarkable talent in carving wood sculptures. You might like to take them to your room and show them what you have done."

Christopher's pale face flooded with pink. "I am not very good as I wish," he said. "It makes me shame for showing them now. I have not done such work before."

"We would like to see them," Laura said. "And then afterwards, perhaps Dr. Bartlett will let you have dinner with us at the inn. We'll bring him back early, Dr. Bartlett."

"Of course," the headmaster said. He rose, relieved. "I'll leave you to yourselves, then, Mrs. Winters. We like the boys to be in the dormitory by ten o'clock, but since it's holiday time, we shan't be too strict."

"We'll have him back before ten," Chris said. "I'm weary, myself."

"You put on a great campaign. I congratulate you on your victory."

Chris smiled. "Trouble's just beginning, I daresay. I have messes to clear up in our city and promises to keep."

"You will do both, I am sure," Dr. Bartlett said gracefully, and withdrew.

Chris rose. "Come along, Boy! Let's see what you are doing. Lead the way for us."

They followed him, and he walked, as Laura observed, with a peculiar grace, an Asian grace, for it was her remembered impression that all Koreans walked with that smooth step, each foot exactly placed. His head was well set, the dark straight hair lying neatly to the skull, and yet the shape of the body was American, Western, strong, the frame not slight, the bones well articulated, the hands not small. She had an opportunity to see those hands at work a few minutes later when they were in Christopher's room, for he drew aside a curtain from a box that stood upended in one corner of the room. There revealed was a miniature family sitting room, a comfortable room designed, as she saw, after the room they had just left, with a settee, chairs, and round tables. In the chairs sat two figures, a man and a woman, the man reading a book, the woman sewing. She recognized them as resembling herself and Chris.

"Christopher," she exclaimed, "how clever they are! See, Chris, the man actually looks like you."

She took the figure in her hands. It stood perhaps seven inches high, and every detail was clear, the wide-set eyes, the smooth hair, real hair, she saw, glued on hair by hair, and the garments exact and neatly made.

"Good work," Chris said. He had a strange feeling, not quite comfortable, of recognizing himself in this puppet.

The boy did not answer. He accepted the praise without a smile, and when they had seen everything, exclaiming over this and that, he drew the curtain again.

"So this is where you live and sleep," Laura said, looking about the room.

"Here is my half, there is John's," Christopher said.

"The two halves are quite different," she went on. "I can tell the difference between you."

Two aspects of one room, and yet there was no mistaking which side was Christopher's. On one side there were pennants and pinups, not of girls but of jet aircraft and nuclear weapons. On the other, the walls were bare except for a stark small drawing of a mountain rising above clouds.

"Yours?" she asked, and Christopher nodded.

She turned to Chris. "We have an artist."

"Most boys are artists for a while," he retorted. "I used to draw ships, and my mother was all excited about them."

Something cool crept into the atmosphere and Laura dispelled it promptly.

"Let's have dinner," she said. "I'm hungry."

"Well, what do you think?" she asked the next morning in their hotel bedroom as she dressed.

"Too quiet," Chris said.

She turned on him with indignation. "Of course he's quiet! He doesn't know what will happen to him."

Chris, still in his pajamas, stretched himself on one of the two beds. "Do we know?"

She corrected him. "Do *you* know? It's for you to decide, not me! Whatever you decide I'll follow faithfully, but I will not decide."

"What would you do, imagining you were in my place?"

"I can't imagine it," she said, so promptly that he laughed.

"I shouldn't have left myself open for that! Don't think I'm not puzzling, Laura. Don't think I'm immune to the fact that the boy's my son, either. But the arguments still hold. Maybe when I've proved myself a great governor, maybe then we can introduce him gradually into our lives. After all, the times are loosening up. Plenty of half-American kids over there and people are beginning to know it. But just at this moment, when I haven't stabilized my public image, it would be suicide. Timing is everything. Give me time."

"The boy is growing up very fast, Chris. He's thinking and feeling. His soul is crystallizing. Some day soon it may be too late."

"What do you mean, too late?"

"We may not be able to reach him if we wait too long. He'll reject us, because he'll know we've rejected him."

"Oh, come now, Laura, these are old, worn-out words. Psychiatrists have taken all the gloss off them long ago. He has to realize that he's in circumstances that may be peculiar—at least unusual—but he has to accept them. He'll have to explain over and over again in his lifetime who he is, even to himself. He's born, he exists, he's different. The sooner he accepts himself, the better for him. Even if he came into our home today, he would not be the child we might have had together, you and I."

"No, but we could help him accept himself by accepting him ourselves."

"Have you decided already what should be done, in spite of saying that you won't make the decision?"

She retreated. "No, I'm only arguing on both sides. I might say, on the other hand, that it would be simpler for him if he did not have to explain *us,* and therefore he's better off alone."

"He's not alone."

"Yes, he is, in all essentials."

"No more than every one is, basically."

"Not at his age, and from a far country."

"We'd better send him back, you're saying—decision again!"

"We can't send him back. Even if we sent him back physically, he would not be the same boy. Part of him is now here. He knows you are his father. He'd be strange in Korea. He always was, because people there didn't want him, but now he knows it. He didn't before. The rope has been cut, Chris. He's out in the middle of the ocean, looking for the shore."

Chris leaped from the bed. "Let's just enjoy the skiing today, shall we?"

It was not difficult. The day was brilliantly clear and cold, the air windless, the snow perfect. They breakfasted and then found Christopher, waiting and ready, in the entrance to the main building, skis in hand. He had a look of cautious excitement, the air of a child who had known disappointment, and in the midst of hope was also ready for despair. But he was handsome, she thought, his eyes the dark violet blue that was so strange a mixture, his olive skin smooth and clear against the red of an old parka. He would have his problems with women someday, that was to be foretold, and could the chance of his birth keep him from a woman whom he might love? Foolish to let her mind leap ahead of the years!

"You like to ski, Boy?" Chris asked. Laura had a peculiar feeling that the word "son" was very close, and her heart leaped for a second; but he substituted the lesser word, for the present at least, or perhaps forever?

"I like," Christopher answered, "but not most."

"What do you like most?" Laura asked.

They were out to the car now, settling skis upon the rack. Then they got in, Christopher alone in the back seat.

"So what do you like most?" Laura repeated.

He considered carefully. This human being, she thought, would never answer any question quickly. There was a deep caution in him, a disbelief in life.

"I like best singing," he said at last.

"Sing to us," she said. "We've never heard you. We didn't even know you could sing."

He considered a moment, then without comment he lifted his head and sang a Korean song. They listened, exchanging looks. This was no ordinary singing, a music as clear as a flute, the voice still unchanged, a high soprano but not thin. There was power in this voice. Chris, she wanted to cry, can this boy be wasted? But she remained silent and when he had finished she said "Thank you," and since Chris was silent, too, she was about to say "Let's get on with the skiing," when suddenly he spoke.

"Let's hear an American song, Boy."

Without hesitation Christopher began again to sing. "Oh, beautiful for spacious skies—"

He sang the entire song, Chris driving straight ahead as he listened, his eyes fixed on the road and the snow-covered mountains beyond. When the voice ceased he did not speak for a moment. Then he said, "I like that one, Boy. I'm glad you know that one."

Neither speech nor song for the next ten miles, until they came to the mountain and to the ski slopes, and then there was no time for anything except the preparation for the sport, the strapping on of skis, the seating in the ski lift and rising up over the white flanks, until the lift stopped and deposited them on the crest of the mountain.

"You ski between us, Boy," Chris said, "and Laura goes first. I'll follow so that I can pick up pieces, if necessary."

He was very busy checking straps and equipment, obviously nervous about the boy and, not knowing his skills, ready with advice. "Sure you know how to turn? Watch Laura—yes, call her Laura—I give my permission and you may call me Chris if you like. We're all friends, aren't we? So, here we go!"

They were off, and she dared not turn her head until they were at the foot of the first steep slope. Then, slowing, she looked behind her up at the mountain. Christopher was making a slalom, cautiously resolute and with perfect form, and farther up the mountain Chris was gathering speed. They met at the foot of the mountain, their cheeks red with cold and their eyes bright with warmth. Chris had forgotten all problems. He clapped Christopher's shoulder.

"You'll make a famous skier, Boy!" he shouted.

"Thank you, Father," Christopher replied.

Their eyes met, Chris amused and somewhat embarrassed, the boy unsmiling.

"All right," Chris said.

It was impossible not to yield to Christmas. They had bought nothing for themselves or for Christopher, Christmas until now an unreality in the shadow of immensities of decisions and resolutions. Now these faded away in the brilliant snow-lit sunshine of one bright day after another, and Christmas itself came near.

"The boy needs better skis," Chris declared one morning while they were dressing. "I'll get them for his Christmas, and I'll show him how to take care of them."

"And I shall buy him a new parka," Laura said. "The one he's wearing is something left behind by an old boy. It's all right, but it's not his. And he needs better carving tools. I saw a set from Denmark the other day in that specialty shop on the corner."

Once they began to prepare for Christmas there was no stopping the rising flood of enjoyment, as old as tradition itself. Chris had long been cynical, declaring that cities and merchants had made a commercial circus of the whole day. Here, however, in the simplicities of the small clusters of houses and shops of a mountain village, there was no false glitter. Christmas trees were cut by fathers and sons and decorated by the family, and Chris, to Laura's amazement, declared on the morning of Christmas Eve that he and Christopher must ascend the low hill behind the school and choose an appropriate tree. The three of them would decorate it, and Laura must find the ornaments. While they were gone she searched for the unusual, and liking a tree sparely trimmed she brought back her choices and waited for the return. In an hour they returned, "my men," as she called them in her thoughts, and Chris put the tree into a frame he made for its base, and she began to hang the ornaments. Christopher had never seen a Christmas tree, but as he sat cross-legged on the floor watching her, he reached for the silver and gold paper in which the ornaments had been wrapped, and began to fashion them into the shapes of butterflies and birds.

"Lovely," Laura said. "Let's hang them on the tree, too."

And Chris, lounging now in a comfortable smoking jacket, watched the two of them, thinking, thinking, his mind playing upon possibilities. Possibilities, not all impossibilities! Now Laura could see this in his eyes, could feel it in his smile. Perhaps, she thought, for the first time a resolution of their problem loomed in the near distance. Once Christmas was over, once he was home again, perhaps he'd be ready to let the decisive impulse appear.

Well, this was Christmas time, and while he always proclaimed that he had no sentimentalities, he was obviously allowing himself to be amused by Christmas in a village as like a Christmas card as could be imagined. Christmas lights lit up the fir trees that stood outside the houses, snow fell freshly on Christmas Eve, was falling at this very moment while Christopher and Laura trimmed the tree which he had set up in a corner of the sitting room of their suite here in the small, clean hotel. It was the boy's first Christmas, and he watched Christopher while Laura told him the Christmas story.

"It is the birthday of a great and good man, so good that he called himself, and was called by other people, the Son of God."

Christopher listened carefully, sitting cross-legged near the tree, now shining with pointed lights.

"What is God?" he asked.

"Have they not told you here at school?" Laura asked.

"I hear the name," he said.

"The Name is all we know," Laura said. "No one has seen his face. We can only talk of him and believe that he exists because the worlds exist and somehow they were made. But this one who called himself the Son was born on Earth—"

She told the old story, and Christopher listened with increasing intensity.

"And so the Son had nowhere to lay his head," she finished softly.

Christopher sighed, he clasped his arms and rocked himself back and forth. "Sometimes I, too, had nowhere to lay the head. Sometimes my grandmother was angry to me, and I must run away and at night put my head on the street to sleep."

She met Chris's eyes with eloquent inquiry. Can we return him to that?

The day had proceeded to evening and they were busy with wrapping gifts, each in turn putting his gifts beneath the tree. Every move was new to Christopher and exciting. His face had lost its habitual look of gravity. His eyes sparkled, those eyes which looked black and were blue. He forgot to be dignified and he laughed and poured out questions.

"Like this? Like this?"

He was wrapping a small box.

"Like that," Chris said. "Now put the card on with the name of the person it's for."

"It's for you," Christopher cried, laughing. "It is for

you only! You will like very much. Shall I show you now?"

"No, no, not until tomorrow morning. Then everyone will open the gifts. It'll be fun."

With these words Christopher was taken by a sudden ecstasy. Chris felt the boy's arms clasp him about his waist. He looked down into the changed face, vivid now with feeling.

"I am liking you too much, my father!"

"It can't be too much, Boy," he said and put his arm about the firm young shoulders.

Then he released himself gently. It could be too much. If he decided to leave the boy here it could indeed be too much.

"It's time we all went to bed," he said. "Nearly midnight—good heavens!"

It was the next morning, however, when he knew it would really be too much, next morning after the breakfast had been sent up to their rooms and been eaten, the Christmas tree blazing away. Breakfast over, the gifts were to be opened and exclaimed upon. In his own pile Chris found a carved box, small but exquisite, that Christopher had made.

"For me, first," he said frankly, "for putting stamps in, but I wish to give you."

"I need just such a box for my collar buttons," Chris said.

But Christopher was already absorbed in a joy of his own, his new skis.

"For me?" he asked. "Only for me?"

Assured, he was compelled to put on new boots and strap on the skis and time passed, and when the church bells rang for morning service not all the gifts were opened and they must hurry, for Christopher sang in the choir. Out into the fresh snow again they went, wrapped against the keen morning wind that blew snow into their faces. They walked a few blocks down the street, now gay with people, and filed into the church among the crowd. Christopher left them then and tiptoed into the vestry, and there among the other boys from the village and school he donned his white robe and marched into the choir loft. Then he searched the congregation until he found the two to whom he somehow belonged, though in what way he did not know, and he continued to watch them until the moment came, just before the sermon, when he had his solo to sing. Now he rose, stepped forward to the edge of the loft, and his hands clasped behind his back, he began to sing as he had never sung before.

"What child is this—"

His voice soared into the groined ceiling and Laura, sitting hand in hand with Chris, released herself, and opening her bag she felt for her handkerchief. Chris, hearing a soft sob, turned his head to look at her, and met her eyes, wet with tears.

"Chris," she whispered. "What child indeed—what child is this?"

He made no answer.

"Do you want to talk with Henry Allen?" Laura asked.

Christmas was over and they were home again but she knew that Chris was very far away, wandering somewhere in a country of his own. They had not talked beyond the needs of daily living, not for the four days since they returned. He had been busy at his office, preparatory to moving into the Capitol buildings, and she too was preparing for the move. This house, which was their true home and would always be, would be left exactly as it was, with Greta to be the caretaker. Weekends and holidays they would come home, but the work week must be elsewhere, beginning next week. For years it had been their habit to give a great party for all their friends, this on New Year's Eve, and tomorrow was the next to their last day.

Chris did not reply. They were alone, a rare and treasured evening of which there could only be a few, henceforth. The wood fire was burning in the chimneypiece here in their own sitting room upstairs, and she sat in her rose-red velvet chair, Chris opposite her, in his blue smoking jacket. When he did not answer she went on with her needlepoint, an ancient work which she had begun years before and now picked up of an evening without intent or even much hope of ever finishing, but it gave her hands something to do when she could not read, if she were alone with Chris.

When still he did not reply she spoke again, "I know you are troubling your mind over something and I can guess it's about Christopher. Right?"

"Right."

"So if you don't want to talk with me—and I can understand that because you think I'm biased in his favor —then why not Henry Allen?"

"I make my own decisions," Chris said.

She was silent for a moment, putting her needle in and out with a resolute calm. What was he thinking? She felt far from him, pushed away, set aside, and that strange foolish jealousy hovered once again in the offing of her spirit. Was he with Soonya? Were Soonya, Christopher and he together now in his thoughts? She sighed and folded her work.

"I think I'll go to bed. I feel weary tonight."

"You're not ill?"

"No. Perhaps I need to get back to my own work."

"That work of yours—it's your escape."

"Maybe. We all need an escape, don't we, Chris?"

Her voice was cool, she meant it to be so, and he felt the coolness and caught her hand as she passed. "Don't be cross with me, sweet!"

"Of course not. Only—I'm so long in the dark."

"I have to do this my own way."

"You've always done things your own way, haven't you, Chris?"

"But you want that, surely?"

She had the impulse to withdraw her hand, being so very far away, but she did not. Instead she sat down on the footstool by his chair.

"I do want it, usually," she said. "Haven't I always wanted you to be free? But where this child is concerned, somehow I feel I have a right to know what is going on in your mind. In a sense, he's my child now, too. He has no mother but me. When I took him away from—from Soonya—which I could never have done, Chris, if I'd thought she loved him or ever could love him—no, truly, I couldn't have—I assumed the responsibility of being his mother—another sort of mother, of course, a woman who only took the place of someone else, but someone he'd really never had. So yes, in a sense I do feel you owe it to me at least to share your thoughts."

He listened, his blue eyes shining like hard sunlight upon her face upturned to his. But he shook his head.

"Sorry," he said shortly. "I still can't. I've got to decide on what it means to me, one way or the other. I don't know which way, but I'm plugging along, step by step, toward some end or other. It's my career, my life."

"Henry Allen—" she interrupted.

"Not Henry Allen's,'" he retorted.

She gazed up into those blue eyes and saw herself reflected very small in the black pupils. "Does it occur to you that if you decide one way I may—despise you?"

"So be it," he said grimly.

She rose and kissed him lightly on the forehead and went to her own room. There she stood, hesitant for a moment. Then she went to the door between their rooms, standing open as it usually did, and she closed it firmly and locked it. She stood another instant. Then she unlocked it, but left it closed.

Two nights later and the house was filled with the noise and laughter of their party. The swaying music of a dance band drifted through the open rooms. She had chosen to decorate the rooms in smart modern flower arrangements, and guests in clusters were admiring what she had done.

She enjoyed such decorative effects and planning them with a florist had occupied her surface mind while she waited, for what she did not know. There had been no letter from Christopher—Kim Christopher, she was beginning to call him again in her thoughts, for a reason only intuitive or perhaps only defensive, perparing herself for Chris if he decided—

"How do you do, Laura," Mrs. Allen said.

She turned to greet them both, Mr. and Mrs. Henry Allen, Mrs. Allen in her usual black taffeta, and he in the dinner jacket he had had made in London years ago, which stretched across his now expanding front in concentric wrinkles.

"You're looking beautiful in that white gown, my dear," she said, pressing Laura's hand. "But everything is even more splendid than usual. I shan't like not coming to this party next year."

"Ah, but you will come," she said impetuously. "We shall have it every year as usual, forever!"

They smiled and went on and she turned to other guests, other couples, gathering thickly now in the three great rooms. In the dining room, waiters were standing ready to serve at the loaded buffet tables, in the drawing room people were already dancing, here in the library she and Chris—where was Chris? A moment ago he had been in the room and coming, she supposed, to stand at her side. Now he was gone. She turned her head this way and that. No, he was not to be seen. Ah, he must be with Berman in his study. O Chris, can't you forget business for a moment? she muttered between her teeth. She longed to find him instantly and then could not, the guests were coming too fast.

"Where's Chris?"

"I don't see Mr. Winters."

Again and again she parried. "He's here somewhere. I'll find him in a moment."

Then suddenly he was there again. He entered from the hall, looking very confident and strong, his cheeks red as though he had been outdoors. He came to her side at once.

"Chris, where have you been?"

"You'll know later."

There was no time for more between them. The evening caught them into its whirl. "A wonderful party, you do everything well," he told her fondly as they danced. Then someone cut in and she did not see him again except here and there, now dancing, now talking, now playing the host with his usual ease. All the guests were here, two hundred perhaps, she guessed, almost as many as they had invited. She glanced at the clock now and again. Half an hour until midnight and the new year! It was always a solemn moment, this midnight of the passing year, but never as solemn as upon this night. The new year—what did it hold? The old question posed itself and she slipped into the small conservatory for a moment alone. There was more in this year to come than the new life for Chris as governor, more for her than being his wife and the first lady. This year would answer her question about Chris. Whatever he did she would love him, but was that love quite enough? Either for him or for her? What if there were that certain loss which she so dreaded? What if he did not rise to the full height she set for him?

And wrong of me, she thought, because when I set a height of my own for him, I make a decision for him which I have no right to make.

Suddenly there was a stir at the door leading into the hall. The band stopped playing. But it was too soon, wasn't it? Not yet midnight—and usually the dance always went on at a quickening pace until the hour struck and the music broke into Auld Lang Syne.

"My friends!"

Chris was standing at the open door from the hall and his voice rang through the rooms. She came out from behind the greenery but she did not enter the crowded rooms. She had never seen him look like this, not even when he made his acceptance speech as the new governor.

"I speak to you as my friends," he was saying. "I speak to you, too, as men and women who have supported me in my ambition to be the governor of our state. I will not, indeed, I could not, hide from you what it means to me to have reached this point. Yes, I'm ambitious! Yes, I have my dreams! I shall continue to dream. I want to be a good governor. I want to serve you and all our people well. I believe I can. But tonight I want to share with you a part of my life of which you have known nothing."

She knew instantly what he was about to do, and she listened, her breath tight in her throat, tears streaming down her cheeks, her heart beating its drums. She listened while he painted in powerful strokes the description of young men far from home, lost in wars they did not understand, fighting battles with enemies human and inhuman.

"These are our men," he said. "They are our sons and brothers. They are living and dying today in seven countries of Asia! They are very young, pitifully young. They grew up in homes like yours and mine—kindly, warm, safe homes. Today they feel utterly alone. How do I know? Because I was one of them once, long ago, in a country called Korea."

He paused and pressed his lips together and went on. "Our young men find what comfort they can, wherever they can. I neither blame nor defend them. I was one of them. They clutch at life with both hands, for they never know what hour they must die. I was one of them. They gather in dance halls. There is no other place to gather. They meet girls. They buy what love they can find. Yes, they know it is a pitiful, tawdry kind of love, but it is usually all that is to be had. They live in the shadow of impending death and they seek refuge in the arms of a girl—a stranger, but a woman. I was one of those young men, but luckier than most, for what I found, though temporary, was not tawdry. But the story does not end there. If it did it would not be worth telling. Again and again it does not end there. From that brief union, which so often ends in tomorrow's death, some times there comes a life. It is the life of a child. In those seven countries of Asia where our men are living, fighting, dying today, these children are being born. What significance have they? This—they are the new people, children of the future, born too soon, before the world is ready for them. No one is ready for them, no country, no man, no woman. They are born stateless. Do the fathers know? Sometimes they do, sometimes they do not. What they don't know is that in Asia the child belongs to the father. I was one of those who did not know—until such a child was born to me. Now I know."

He paused in a long silence, an endless silence, she thought. He was gazing high over their heads, his jaw set. She knew the pulse that was beating in that firm jaw. The room was utterly silent—not a movement, nor a cough, not a whisper. Now he turned and put out his hand, and she saw him draw Christopher into the room. They stood side by side, father and son. The son looked up at the father, and the father smiled down at the son. Impossible not to see the resemblance—the same eyes, the same mouth, the same profile!

"Christopher," Chris said, "these are our friends. I want you to know them and I want them to know you because you are home now to stay. I want them to know me, too. That's why I tell them about you."

The boy did not move. He continued to look up at his father. Chris was speaking to the people again, this time gaily as though he were suddenly released. "Friends, this is my son—our son, for my wife is with me in all this. She went to Korea and brought our boy back with her, our son Christopher. He has a beautiful voice. I want him to sing for you. Sing, Christopher!"

Christopher stepped forward then, one step in front of his father, and lifting his head he sang:

"My country, 'tis of thee—"

O Chris, Laura was crying softly to herself, O Chris, who but you—who but you—

She must get control quickly now, for as soon as the song was ended, she must be there beside them. But she was not quick enough. Before she reached them old Mr. and Mrs. Allen swept forward, arm in arm.

"Welcome, Christopher," Mrs. Allen said in her loud imperial voice. "We're glad you've come home."

"Welcome, my boy," Mr. Allen said and seizing Christopher's two hands in his he shook them both at the same time. Then he turned to Chris. "Congratulations, Winters, a fine son—very fine boy—glad you found him— glad about—everything!"

The crowd waited, doubtful, then surged forward to follow the old pair who had always been their leaders. And Laura, running through the hall, took her place beside Chris. In the midst of handshaking, curious looks, and various smiles, she found a chance to whisper.

"What next, Chris, my love?"

He gave her his one-sided smile. "Who knows?"

"Anyway," she whispered, "there are three of us now."

"So far, so good," he said.

"So far, so good," she echoed, and behind his back she reached for Christopher's right hand.

As the clock began to strike that magic hour the voices of their friends around them rose in song. Over the singing could be heard the clear bell-toned voice of their child Christopher—"Should auld acquaintance be forgot . . ." Never, she thought, never forgotten! But Soonya, Mr. Choe, Korea, were all a part of the past, and this was a new year.

COLOPHON

This is one of the titles in a series of the Oriental Novels of Pearl S. Buck. Other titles include *All Men Are Brothers*, *Dragon Seed, East Wind: West Wind, The Good Earth, A House Divided, Imperial Woman, Kinfolk, The Living Reed, Mandala, The Mother, Pavilion of Women, Peony, The Promise, Sons,* and *Three Daughters of Madame Liang.*

The text was set in Granjon. The typeface was designed by George William Jones (1860-1942) and named after the famous Parisian punch-cutter, Robert Granjon (1513-1589). This face was the model for such popular faces as Times New Roman, Plantin, and Galliard, and was originally designed to compete with Monotype Garamond. The display face is Calligraphy 421 with the folios in Sabon.

This book was typeset by Rhode Island Book Composition, Kingston, Rhode Island and printed by Versa Press, Peoria, Illinois on acid free paper. ∞